A real bad mother . . .

"This is the first of October," Ma Purdy said, "an' I hear tell that the first of ever' month is payday for your stagecoach employees. There ought to be a king's ransom on that coach."

Shottish heard the click of the fat lady's gun cocking behind his head.

"Under the forward seat! The money's there!" he blurted out.

Two of her sons immediately jumped into the stagecoach and ripped up the front seat. Then Sherman came out, proudly holding up a black valise. He threw it on the ground at his mother's feet.

She shot off the lock and said to Digger, her youngest, "Count it, sonny."

Digger emptied the bag and sifted through its contents. "Money's good."

"Damn right," Ma said, then turned to Shottish. "I told you not to lie to me."

Seeing what was coming, the man begged, "No, please! I have children and a wife!"

Ma said, "Got kids myself. You have my sympathies."

And then she pulled the trigger. . . .

THE TRAILSMAN

#230

FLATWATER FIREBRAND

by

Jon Sharpe

A SIGNET BOOK

SIGNET
Published by New American Library, a division of
Penguin Putnam Inc., 375 Hudson Street,
New York, New York 10014, U.S.A.
Penguin Books Ltd, 27 Wrights Lane,
London W8 5TZ, England
Penguin Books Australia Ltd,
Ringwood, Victoria, Australia
Penguin Books Canada Ltd, 10 Alcorn Avenue,
Toronto, Ontario, Canada M4V 3B2
Penguin Books (N.Z.) Ltd, 182–190 Wairau Road,
Auckland 10, New Zealand

Penguin Books Ltd, Registered Offices:
Harmondsworth, Middlesex, England

First published by Signet, an imprint of New American Library,
a division of Penguin Putnam Inc.

First Printing, December 2000
10 9 8 7 6 5 4 3 2 1

The first chapter of this book originally appeared in *Manitoba Marauders*,
the two hundred twenty-ninth volume in this series.

 REGISTERED TRADEMARK—MARCA REGISTRADA

Printed in the United States of America

PUBLISHER'S NOTE
This is a work of fiction. Names, characters, places, and incidents either are
the product of the author's imagination or are used fictitiously, and any
resemblance to actual persons, living or dead, events, or locales is entirely
coincidental.

The Trailsman

Beginnings . . . they bend the tree and they mark the man. Skye Fargo was born when he was eighteen. Terror was his midwife, vengeance his first cry. Killing spawned Skye Fargo, ruthless, cold-blooded murder. Out of the acrid smoke of gunpowder still hanging in the air, he rose, cried out a promise never forgotten.

The Trailsman they began to call him all across the West: searcher, scout, hunter, the man who could see where others only looked, his skills for hire but not his soul, the man who lived each day to the fullest, yet trailed each tomorrow. Skye Fargo, the Trailsman, and the seeker who could take the wildness of a land and the wanting of a woman and make them his own.

Western Missouri, 1862—Where rails of iron hold family lines together, and hot lead awaits those who dare cross them.

1

Pooter McCoy was drinking straight from the bottle now, and it wasn't making him any nicer.

Skye Fargo peered over the rim of his whiskey glass as he downed the last of the rotgut, his gaze fixed on the skinny little weasel who was dealing stud at a table a dozen or so yards away. They were in a saloon called the Buffalo Chip, in the town of Flatwater, Nebraska Territory.

Pooter McCoy stood about five feet six inches and weighed less than a damp ironing board. His hair was like straw, his chest sunken, his forehead high, and Fargo figured he could count McCoy's teeth on the fingers of one hand. His eyes were closer together than any eyes had a right to be. Pooter McCoy was doubtless the product of kissin' cousins.

The town of Salinas, Kansas, wanted McCoy for slaughtering two innocent souls in a poorly planned bank robbery, in which McCoy's brother, Bug, was also killed. Pooter drilled the clerk with lead and, in the confusion, a parson's wife who just happened to scream at the wrong moment.

Pooter McCoy escaped without a penny, but escape he did. There was blood on his hands and a price on his head, a very tidy thousand dollars. With some careful arithmetic, Fargo reasoned, he could live fairly comfortably for several months on a thousand. But if women and whiskey were involved, and they usually were, the reward would last a few weeks.

Fargo had picked up McCoy's trail a little south of Omaha and tracked him all the way here. Fargo's journey was ten days old, and he was ready to end it, then sleep until his next birthday. He placed his shot glass back on the bar.

The bartender, a tubby sort of a fellow, asked, "Again?"

Fargo nodded. Filling the glass, the bartender commented, "Smells like snow."

Fargo said, "This town smells like a lot of things, but snow ain't one of them." The bartender grunted something, scooped some wet coins off the bar, and went away.

Fargo watched as McCoy started dealing the next hand—from the bottom, not surprisingly—taking a long swig from the bottle after the last card was dealt. With him at the table were a couple of local cowboys and a citified dandy in a dusty suit and derby hat. A drummer most likely, from back East. The locals didn't seem to notice McCoy's sloppy cheating methods, probably because they were as sloshed as he was. The drummer, though, looked frightened. Like Fargo, he had doubtless seen his share of inbred, neck-bowed hard cases like Pooter McCoy, men with a low tolerance for whiskey and a high one for violence.

The drummer wisely threw in his cards after the hand was dealt and said, "Too rich for my blood." He hastily grabbed his money from the table and made his way to the bar, where he ordered a whiskey.

The drummer said to Fargo, "Man would be a fool to stay in that game."

Fargo said nothing, watching McCoy win another hand. He took another healthy slug from the bottle and let out a belch that echoed into the next territory. It was just a matter of time before the cowboys got wise to McCoy's half-assed card tricks, and then all hell would break loose. Fargo hoped to avoid this.

The drummer said, "If you were thinking about getting into that game, mister, I'd strongly advise against it. Not only is that boy a piss-poor cheater, my innards tell me he's prone to violence."

"You reckon?" Fargo asked.

"In my line of work," the drummer said, motioning for a refill, "I can smell trouble a mile away. Pure Arkansas trash, that one."

"He's from Missouri," Fargo said.

The drummer went on, "Crimp's the name, Hiram Crimp. Armstrong Anvil Company, Pittsburgh, Pennsylvania. And a better judge of character you'll not meet."

Fargo watched as McCoy sucked down the last of the backwash in the bottle and hollered for another. The bartender seemed reluctant to bring it, knowing that little good would come from Pooter McCoy having more to drink.

Fargo saved him the trouble. He slapped a silver dollar on the bar and said to the bartender, "Let me buy the lad a drink."

The bartender looked uncertain until McCoy flung the empty whiskey bottle across the saloon, where it missed the piano player by a good inch and a half, shattering against the wall. "Bring me another bottle, dammit, or I'll blow yer head off!" McCoy shouted.

What happened next would become the stuff of legend in Nebraska Territory for decades to come and make the Buffalo Chip Saloon a landmark.

Fargo took the full whiskey bottle from the bartender and uncorked it, never taking his eyes off Pooter McCoy. The bartender said to Fargo, "I hope you know what you're doing, friend."

"So do I," Fargo replied, grabbing a couple of glasses off the bar.

"Sir, as I said—" Hiram Crimp began.

"I know," Fargo said, walking slowly toward McCoy and the cowboys. "A better judge of character I'll never find."

As he walked, Fargo planned his next move. McCoy wouldn't be taken alive, of that Fargo was sure, but he had to at least try. And the cowboys at the poker table would have to go, and quickly.

Clutching the whiskey bottle and the glasses, Fargo sat down at the table and said, "Mind if I join in?"

Even drunk, Pooter McCoy's lifeless black orbs burned with suspicion. Before he could answer, Fargo poured him a drink, then one for himself. The cowboys, who couldn't have been older than eighteen, pushed their empty whiskey glasses toward Fargo, licking their lips.

"You boys are too young to drink," Fargo said to them.

One of them opened his mouth in angry protest. Fargo shot him a stare that shut him up quick. The boys took the hint, scooping up their money and bidding their farewells.

"Looks like it's just you and me," Fargo said. He raised his glass to McCoy and added, "To your health, Mr. McCoy."

McCoy was quick. Crying out in a ferocious animal

4

yowl, he dropped the whiskey glass, which was halfway to his bloodless lips, and kicked back from the table, starting to rise and go for the holster on his right hip.

Fargo upended the table right into McCoy, sending cards, glasses, and poker chips flying. Fargo was on his feet and reaching for the Colt and, in that next split second, was horrified to see that McCoy was up and had somehow sidestepped the poker table. He was also clearing leather. He fired once at Fargo, who was already diving to his left, out of the line of fire. The bullet whizzed by him; Fargo heard a distinctively wet splat. McCoy cried out again, a bloodcurdling shriek of hate and anger. In the years to come, bartender Eustace McGonigle would describe it to customers as "the most god-awful, inhuman sound these ears have ever heard, or ever will hear."

Fargo hit the floor, rolled once, and was up. The Colt was rock steady in his hand. He fired, and the bullet cut a wide, deep-crimson swath against the side of McCoy's head, taking the best part of his right ear with it. McCoy cried out in pain and fired back wildly, the blood in his eyes momentarily blinding him. Fargo dodged again, but was up before McCoy could blink a third time. Fargo aimed and squeezed off another shot, and this time hit pay dirt. The bullet smashed into McCoy's cheek half an inch below the eye and blew out the back of his head.

McCoy dropped like a sack of brass doorknobs. For a moment there was absolute silence, then the piano player moaned and fainted dead away, collapsing off his stool into a heap on the sawdust-covered floor.

"Shit on fire and save the matches," Eustace McGonigle muttered in a small voice.

Fargo made his way over to McCoy's lifeless carcass and prodded him with his boot. It never hurt to be sure. He looked down at the gaping hole in McCoy's head, thick black blood oozing like molasses. Pooter McCoy wouldn't be shooting another pastor's wife anytime soon.

"I was hopin' to take him alive," Fargo said, to no one in particular.

"Your secret's safe with me, mister," McGonigle said.

Fargo vaguely heard the bartender offer him a drink, heard the sound of a glass and a fresh bottle being placed on the bar. He did hear McGonigle comment, "Sweet limpin' Jesus, lookit what we got here."

Fargo looked. Lying at the floor at the base of the bar, a bullet between his eyes, was Hiram Crimp, late of the Armstrong Anvil Company, Pittsburgh, Pennsylvania. His eyes were wide open, but he was as dead as dead ever gets.

"Damn," Fargo said.

He really needed that drink.

Eustace McGonigle went to get the town marshal. A minute or two later, he was back, accompanied by a bear of a man with a bushy black moustache, even bushier black eyebrows, and a generally angry countenance. He was bigger than Fargo by four inches and fifty pounds. A dented tin star was pinned to his vest.

He looked at Pooter McCoy, then at Hiram Crimp. He said to Fargo, "This better be good."

Fargo finished his whiskey. He said, "I think you'll like it."

The marshal motioned to McCoy's body, which was

already drawing flies. He said, "You know him, or was he dealing with a hot deck?"

"Both," Fargo said. "Name's Pooter McCoy. He's wanted for some murders back to Salinas. I was sort of hoping this wouldn't happen."

"And this one?" the marshal asked, pointing to Hiram Crimp.

"Wrong saloon in the wrong town on the wrong day."

"It's my hope," the marshal said, "that you got some proof that this Pooter McCoy has a price on his head."

"Wanted poster's in my saddlebag," Fargo said.

"You got a name?" the marshal asked.

"Fargo. Skye Fargo."

The marshal looked thoughtful for a moment. He said, "Fargo, huh? I heard tell of you." He turned to McGonigle and said, "Eustace, you tend to these dead folks. Go fetch Jacob Belinsky. Me and Mr. Skye Fargo is going to retire to my office for a spell. We got some items to talk about." He said to Fargo, "Anytime you're ready."

"Mind if I have another drink first?"

"Go ahead, you'll probably need it," the marshal said. "What's comin' ain't going to be much fun."

The marshal's name was Deke Thornton. He said, "I got two men layin' dead in the saloon over yonder. That don't make me happy, Fargo."

Thornton was sitting at his battered old desk. Fargo took him to be thirty-six, maybe a bit older. His voice was calm, but Fargo knew instinctively that Thornton was a hell storm just waiting to erupt. He'd met dozens like him over the years—leather-tough, hardworking, essentially honest lawmen who didn't cotton to strangers shooting up their towns. Upon entering the jail, Fargo had been relieved of his weapons, and wisely did not protest.

Fargo was sitting in a rickety chair next to the stove. Thornton didn't seem impressed with the yellowing, dog-eared wanted poster for Pooter McCoy, which sat unfolded on his desk. In fact, he didn't seem to care about it one way or the other.

"You would've had six or seven bodies in the saloon over yonder if I hadn't got McCoy first," Fargo said, not bragging, but just stating the facts. "A real animal. Given the chance, he'd have ventilated everyone in the place. Sorry about the drummer. Seemed like a pleasant enough man."

"That don't make him any less deader," Thornton said. "And he got dead in my town. If there's any killing needed done in Flatwater, I tend to it myself and don't need any strangers doin' my job for me. That makes me look bad, and I won't have that."

Fargo said, "Sorry for making you look bad, Thornton, but I got a living to make."

Thornton was up quickly. His eyes were granite. Pointing a beefy finger in Fargo's face, he yelled, "An innocent man is dead, Fargo, and I'm seriously deciding whether to hold you responsible."

This wasn't going well at all. Fargo said, "I didn't kill him."

"He'd still be alive if you'd checked in with me first like you're supposed to," Thornton countered. "But no, you just charged in with no thought for anyone and started trading lead with a man you knew was madder than a shit-house rat. No, Hiram Crimp didn't die by your gun, but you killed him just the same."

Fargo said, with some heat, "I don't see it that way, Marshal. I tracked Pooter McCoy from hell to breakfast, and I know what he was capable of. Poor Mr. Crimp is a small price to pay for what might've been."

"But we'll never know now, will we?" Thornton said. "And in this case, not knowin's what matters. I just might let you cool your heels behind bars until I decide what to do with you."

"There's still the question of the thousand-dollar bounty on Pooter McCoy," Fargo said. "I'd like to wire the folks in Salinas, let them know the job is done and they owe me."

"Why should they believe you?" Thornton wanted to know.

"They know me as a man of my word," Fargo said. "Bounty hunting isn't usually in my line. I did this as a favor to some people I know."

"Might take a week for that money to come through," Thornton said. "Don't know if I want you around Flatwater that long. Something tells me you're bad luck, Fargo."

"Yeah," Fargo said. "That happens a lot."

"You got any money?" Thornton asked. "I could always get you for vagrancy if you don't."

"I got enough," Fargo said.

Thornton looked slightly disgusted. He lit a cigar. He said, "All right, Fargo. Against my better judgment, you can leave. Go send your wire. But do it before the sun sets, and find another place to hang your hat till your money arrives."

Fargo wasn't keen on being chased out of any town, much less a one-horse hamlet like Flatwater. He said, "I got a pretty good understanding of the law, Thornton, and unless you got cause to hold me for trial—and you don't—I'm free to come or go as I see fit."

Thornton got red in the face and his moustache twitched. His voice low but rock steady, he said, "Don't you talk to me about the law, you son of a bitch. I don't think I like your attitude, neither. So here's the deal, Skye Fargo. Wait here for your blood money if you want, but if I catch you so much as spitting in the street or breakin' wind in public, I'm gonna cloud up and rain all over you."

"I don't suppose there's any point in asking for my weapons back," Fargo said.

"Not a one," Thornton said, puffing on his cigar. The subject was clearly closed.

Fargo got up to leave. There would be time to argue the matter later. He said, "Is it okay if I get something to eat?"

"Be my guest," Thornton said. "Try Emma's café across the street. The special of the day's chili con carne."

"Okay," Fargo said, making his way to the door. "I won't spit in the street, but when it comes to chili, I ain't making any promises about breaking wind in public."

Flatwater, Nebraska Territory, wasn't much of a town as towns go, but this far west, a man couldn't be too particular. The main street, one of three that made up Flatwater, was ankle deep in mud and manure. Fargo walked his Ovaro to the stable and made arrangements to keep him well supplied with oats and hay for a day or two for the sum of fifty cents.

Fargo found himself the unwanted center of attention by the good people of Flatwater as he walked

10

down the wooden plank sidewalk toward the café. He had a pretty good idea why: two folks dead in a saloon shoot-out wasn't an everyday occurrence out here in hailstone and sarsaparilla country. As he passed by Belinsky's Dry Goods store, a very pretty young lady wearing a yellow sunbonnet passed him on the sidewalk and shot him a pearly white smile that made Fargo's heart flutter. He turned to watch her shapely behind as she lifted her dress and crossed the muddy street.

She was too pretty to get away, he decided, and started after her. Before he could go three steps, he tripped over some very worn-out boots that were attached to a grizzled old geezer who was fast asleep on his saddle behind some kegs of nails. Fargo went flying into the street, landing face down in the brown slop.

Fargo sat up and wiped mud off his face. Some toothless old fart, most of his face covered in gray whiskers, was yelling at him for something. Fargo turned to look for the pretty girl. She was standing in front of the café, called Emma's Tasty Food Emporium, giggling at the sight of him covered in mud.

"This just ain't my day," Fargo said to nobody in particular. The geezer was still cackling at him like a bantam rooster.

". . . stumbling around like a blind man, for corn's sake," he babbled. "Ain't you got the sense the Lord gave a goat?"

"Are you addressing me?" Fargo asked, getting hot.

"Damn right I am," the geezer said. "Why don't you watch where I'm going? Coulda broke my damn leg."

"Well now, you didn't do my clothes any good, either, did you?" Fargo barked.

The geezer gave Fargo the once-over and said, "Ain't you the hard case what drilled those dudes in the saloon afore?"

"Good news travels fast," Fargo said, standing up and wiping mud off his pants. The pretty girl had vanished into the afternoon.

"Yeah," the geezer said now. "Ever'one in Flatwater is buzzin' about it."

"They would," Fargo grumbled.

"Seein' how's you damn near killed me," the geezer said, "the least you can do is buy this." He picked up thirty pounds of seasoned leather, something that at one time might have passed for a saddle, and offered it to Fargo.

Fargo said, "A man would have to be pretty desperate to sell his saddle."

"Sold my horse two days ago," the old geezer said, "and my gun went yestiddy, but I'm sober now, the Lord be praised. All I got's this saddle . . . and a mighty empty belly."

Fargo dug deep into his pocket and pulled out some bills. Handing them to the geezer, he said, "Have some supper on me, old-timer. And I mean supper, not dessert that comes in a bottle."

The geezer said, grabbing the money, "That's mighty fine of you, friend, mighty fine. As sure as the good Lord made little green apples, He's makin' a bountiful spot for ye in heaven."

Fargo said, "Kindly tell Him I'm in no hurry to get there."

The geezer wiped his left hand on his filthy pants and stuck it out toward Fargo. "Callahan's the name. Mushy Callahan. Pleased to make your acquaintance, sir. Y'all want the saddle?"

"Keep it," Fargo said. "Looks older than I am."

"It surely is that, son," Mushy said. "Got me through some dark days, like the time I was surrounded by a passel of the most ornery, blood-lustin' Pawnee braves a man was ever cursed to witness. Could tell you stories—"

"Another time," Fargo said. His stomach demanded immediate attention. He turned to go, then said, "Just to keep the record straight, how many Pawnee braves?"

Mushy looked thoughtful. He said, "Dunno. Coulda been two, coulda been twenty. Truth be told, I don't rightly remember."

"See you around, friend," Fargo said, and went off in search of a bath and a shave. Then he was going to eat everything on the café's bill of fare, and seek out that pretty lady.

Emma's Tasty Food Emporium consisted of nine rickety tables, huge slabs of beef hanging in the kitchen, clearly visible through the splintering swinging doors, and a healthy number of hungry flies. But the cooking smelled good. If there was an Emma, Fargo didn't see her. His order was taken by a short, ill-tempered Swede, who asked, "What you want for eats, mister?"

Fargo said, "Steak, and burn it. With potatoes and anything green you got that might've once passed for a vegetable. Beans, too, and biscuits. You got butter that's fresh?"

"It is so fresh you will have to slap it," the Swede said.

"And some apple cobbler and coffee, lots of it," Fargo said.

The Swede nodded and said, "You the one who shoot people in the saloon, ya?"

"Yeah," Fargo said.

"You kill many men, ya?" the Swede asked.

"Only when they needed killing," Fargo said. "I may have to kill another if I don't get fed pretty soon."

The Swede smiled weakly and disappeared into the kitchen. Fargo heard something yelled in Swedish, and seconds later Fargo heard the sounds of beefsteak being slapped onto a sizzling grill and plates rattling.

The place was more or less empty, save for a skinny old pilgrim wolfing down some roasted chicken and dumplings at a corner table. A young lady burst through the swinging doors, carrying a pitcher of water and a plate of biscuits.

Fargo's heart jumped. It was her—the cutie who'd smiled at him and made him fall into the mud. She wasn't the most beautiful woman he'd ever laid eyes on, but she was close. She was a strawberry blonde, with high cheekbones and a smattering of the cutest little freckles on her nose. Her breasts were works of art, pushed up by the tight, faded dress that showed off her tiny waist to excellent advantage.

"Hello," she said cheerily, setting the biscuits down on the table and filling his water glass. "See you got yourself cleaned up."

His appetite forgotten, Fargo said, "Wouldn't be fitting to be anything but clean for such an attractive lady as you."

She giggled. "If that's a line, sir, then it's at least a new one."

"You got a name?" Fargo asked.

"Yes, I do," she said, and went back into the

kitchen. Fargo noticed that the skinny pilgrim had stopped eating and was staring at him. The price of notoriety, Flatwater style, he reasoned. Not much happened in a small town like this; saloon shoot-outs were few and far between. Killing Pooter McCoy would be the talk of the town for months, years even.

The object of Fargo's attention returned, bringing out his first decent meal—he hoped, anyway—in some time. The steak was sufficiently charred on the outside, he could see, and the beans still held some brown, a good sign. Still, it was hard to think about eating when she set the plate down in front of him, just close enough for him to catch a sweet whiff of perfumed soap. Her right breast brushed his check for half a second as she poured his coffee. Fargo's manhood instantly quivered in his buckskins.

"Would you like your cobbler now?" she asked.

"What?" he said, unable to take his eyes off her magnificent breasts.

"I'm up here," she said with a laugh. She was prettier up close. Her lips were made for hot kisses and other sweet things that could get a man arrested in some territories. "I asked if you wanted your cobbler now."

"Anytime is fine," he said, slightly flustered.

He watched her shapely rear vanish back through the swinging doors, his dinner momentarily forgotten. Across the room, the old codger snorted at the sorry spectacle. The lusts of young men amused him. He tossed some coins on the table and shuffled out.

Fargo wrestled with the steak—he'd had worse—and devoured the beans and potatoes, slurping down hot coffee. The waitress returned with the cobbler.

His belly happy now, Fargo got down to the business at hand.

"Given any more thought to telling me your name?" he asked her.

"Not much," she said, but her smile told another story. She wanted to be chased, and Fargo was more than up to the pursuit. "More coffee?"

"Can't hurt to tell a person your name," Fargo said. "How will I know what to call you otherwise?"

A plump, middle-aged, Swedish woman, with her hair in braids, came out of the kitchen wiping her hands on her dirty apron. She barked at the waitress, "You come now, Sarah, and wash dishes, ya?"

"Coming, Aunt Emma," Sarah said. "Will there be anything else?" she asked Fargo.

"Yes," Fargo said. "What time do you get done here?"

"Why do you want to know?"

"I was hoping, ma'am, that maybe I could get to know you better," Fargo said.

"That would hardly be proper," Sarah said. "We haven't been formally introduced, for one thing."

"Skye Fargo, at your service," he said.

"Yes," she said. "So I've heard. That's all anyone is talking about. They say you're a very bad man, Mr. Fargo."

"I'm very nice once you get to know me," he said.

"Sarah!" boomed Aunt Emma's voice from the kitchen. "You do dishes now."

"The white house down the street, on the corner," Sarah said. "Climb the oak tree to the second floor, and slip in the window on the left. Come at midnight. I'll be waiting."

She smiled at him and vanished again, but not before leaving him a check for fifty cents.

Fargo put some money on the table. Whistling happily, he exited Emma's Tasty Food Emporium. The old codger was sitting on a chair outside the café, stuffing a corncob pipe with tobacco.

As Fargo passed, he said, "Something tells me you been gettin' sweet with Ms. Sarah Lundegard."

Fargo answered, "I don't think that's any of your business."

"You seem like a pretty smart feller, Skye Fargo, but you oughta know a couple of things," the oldster said.

The man knew his name. What else was new? "Like what?" Fargo asked, straightening his hat.

"For one thing, that gal's engaged to be married."

"Yeah, well, all's fair in love," Fargo said, walking away.

He was halfway across the street when the codger called out, "And she's engaged to the town marshal, Deke Thornton!"

Fargo stopped dead and turned to the oldster. "Please tell me you're joking, mister."

The oldster chortled gleefully and responded, "Hell, Fargo—I ain't got no sense of humor." He struck a match and lit his pipe, still chuckling as Fargo shook his head sadly, turned, and walked away.

He headed straight for the Buffalo Chip Saloon. Behind him, he heard the codger call out, "Hope you have a real pleasant stay in Flatwater, Skye Fargo!"

Fargo just kept on walking. He wanted some bourbon. Then some more bourbon, and maybe even more after that.

If there had been any bloodshed in the Buffalo Chip a scant few hours earlier, a man would never know it.

The place was pretty much back to normal, with only a few bullet holes in the piano and the wall behind it. Behind the bar, Eustace McGonigle was pouring whiskey and drawing warm beer for the thirsty men of Flatwater. A couple of poker games were in session, all locals this time. The piano player was in full swing, and everyone in the place was talking about this Skye Fargo.

The saloon fell silent when Fargo walked in, all conversation dying in mid syllable. He went to the bar. Eustace McGonigle was in the process of setting down a mug of beer. He saw Fargo, and his hand started shaking, sloshing brew all over the place.

McGonigle said, "We don't want any more trouble, Mr. Fargo."

"Neither do I," he said. "Get me a bottle of whatever passes for your best bourbon."

"Yes, sir," McGonigle responded.

Fargo realized the place was quiet enough to hear a sparrow lay an egg. Worse, most everyone was staring at him.

He said irritably, "Go back to your drinking, for Christ's sake. Am I bothering you?"

People hastily resumed their conversations.

McGonigle placed the bottle and the glass on the bar. He said, "You want I should pour it?"

"Well, it ain't gonna pour its ownself now, is it?" Fargo said lightly.

"Don't expect it would," McGonigle said, nervously pouring bourbon all over the bar but managing to get some into the dirty glass. Fargo chugged it down.

McGonigle said, "Another?"

Fargo said, "What do you think?"

The portly barkeep poured a healthy dollop, which

Fargo disposed of neatly. McGonigle refilled the glass a third time, without being told.

"McGonigle, isn't it?" Fargo asked.

"I'd be bein' Eustace McGonigle, yes, sir."

"They tell me you're a man who can be trusted," Fargo said.

McGonigle thought about it for a bit. He seemed to like the idea. Then he asked, "Begging your pardon, sir, but who would 'they' be?"

"Doesn't matter," Fargo said. "But you are a man who can be trusted, right?"

"Oh, yes, sir, McGonigle said, both proud and a trifle suspicious. "If you don't mind my askin', why would you like to know?"

"There's a little gal works over to Emma's café, name of Sarah," Fargo said.

"Oh, yes, Sarah Lundegard," McGonigle said. "A fine young lass she is. Teaches Sunday school here in town, she does."

Fargo let that pass. He said, "I hear she's going to marry the town marshal, Deke Thornton."

"That's the scuttlebutt, yes, sir," McGonigle answered.

"I see," Fargo said. "Do you have the time, Eustace?"

McGonigle studied Fargo for a moment and said, "If you don't mind my saying so, Mr. Fargo, I believe I know what's on your mind, and if I'm correct, the time may be right for you to stop thinkin' about what you're thinkin' about."

"And I believe I asked you for the time, Eustace," Fargo said.

"Begging your pardon, sir, but Miss Sarah is—"

"The time, Mister McGonigle," Fargo said firmly.

"Eight-fifteen in the evening," McGonigle said.

"Fine," Fargo said. "Now that we've got that settled, would you kindly pour me another blast?"

McGonigle did. He said, "Please don't, Mr. Fargo. Miss Sarah could capture the heart of Saint Peter himself, of that I won't deny. But some wee lasses, when they're young and frisky, well, they're apt to lose their heads when a true man of the West comes to town, and Mr. Thornton, he—"

"Thank you," Fargo said, taking a drink. McGonigle opened his mouth to say something more, but wisely decided against it when Fargo shot him a look. The conversation was over.

McGonigle went away to serve other customers. Fargo drank and pondered things. It had been longer than he cared to remember since he'd sampled a lovely woman's charms. That Sarah Lundegard belonged to Deke Thornton did, however, present a minor dilemma. Getting caught with his pants down would mean a serious problem. Even knowing this, though, Fargo had already made his decision, most likely the moment he'd first laid eyes on her.

He had a few hours to kill before midnight. Certainly enough time for a long hot bath and a shave.

Fargo watched as Deke Thornton tried to put his arm around Sarah Lundegard's shoulders.

Fargo was crouched low behind the east wall of the barn, which faced the nice little two-story frame house where Sarah lived with her aunt and uncle. They'd all come home half an hour earlier. Thornton was already there, waiting for Sarah on the porch swing. Aunt Emma and Uncle Lars disappeared into the house, admonishing Sarah to come to bed soon. Sarah said she would, and settled down on the swing next to Thornton.

They talked, but Fargo was too far way to hear what they were saying. Then Thornton tried to get cozy, attempting to put his arm around her. Sarah was having none of it, removing his arm. They talked more, louder this time, though Fargo could only make out a word here and there.

Then Thornton stood abruptly, and Fargo heard him snap, "Well, maybe you don't want to see me at all."

Sarah snapped back, "Maybe I don't."

"Then maybe I ought to leave," Thornton said, with some heat.

"Perhaps you should," Sarah retorted, and Thornton took her up on the offer. He jumped up from the porch swing, jammed his hat on his head, and disappeared into the cool Nebraska night.

Fargo waited.

Sarah went into the house. Upstairs, he saw dim lamplight appear through the starched curtains, which were billowing in the breeze.

It wasn't quite midnight yet. Fargo forced himself to wait—for about two minutes. He remembered someone saying once, "A man with a stiff pecker throws all caution to the wind."

"Caution be damned," he said to himself, and made his way to the tree beside her bedroom window.

"Good evening, fair maiden," Fargo said, perched on the tree branch outside her window. He took off his hat and bowed as best he could, considering he was twenty feet up. He slipped inside and promptly bumped his noggin loudly on the jamb of the open window.

"Shit," he muttered.

"You do make an elegant entrance, Mr. Fargo," Sarah giggled.

She had made herself remarkably ravishing in a very short time. She stood before him, her feet bare on the thin rug. Her honey-colored hair was down on her shoulders, and she was wearing something silk and frilly that showed off to fine effect her full, ripe body. There was a hint of perfume in the air. Fargo couldn't take his eyes off her.

Sarah picked up the lamp from the night table and blew it out. The room was lousy with moonlight. She put the lamp down, then slowly pushed down the straps of her nightie. She wiggled a few times, and it fell to the floor. Her breasts jutted invitingly, her plump nipples standing at attention in the cool night.

She went to him and curled her arms around his neck, kissing him deeply. He kissed her back and slid his tongue into her mouth; she took it greedily, and surrendered hers in return. His manhood was swollen inside his pants and desperately wanted to get out. Her hand went down to his crotch, and working her way inside, she found what she wanted, and commenced to run her hand up and down his throbbing shaft.

"Oh, Mr. Fargo," she said, her voice low and husky. "Wherever did you get such fine merchandise?"

"It just sorta came with the territory," he said.

Sarah took her leave then, settling seductively on the bed. Fargo attempted to disrobe in less time than a bullet from his Henry rifle took to hit a jackrabbit at fifty paces. He shed his pants and tried to pull off his boots standing up, hopping backward. He lost his balance and grabbed a curtain. He tumbled to the floor, taking the curtain with him, ripping the rod clean off the wall. Sarah gasped and ran toward him.

Fargo stood, struggling to free himself from the fabric, the curtain covering him and making him look like a ghost to any poor, unsuspecting stranger who might have wandered by. He finally shook off the curtain looking slightly sheepish.

"This just isn't my night," Fargo grumbled.

"The night is still young," Sarah said, returning to the bed. "Though I don't exactly know how I'll explain that curtain to Aunt Emma."

"You'll think of something," Fargo said, finishing what he'd started. Soon he was as naked as the day he was born. He joined her on the soft feather bed and took her in his arms, loving the feeling of her firm nipples rubbing against his bare chest. She rolled on top of him, running her fingers through his hair and kissing him hotly, savoring the taste of him. She kissed and licked her way down the length of his body until she reached his hardness. She took it in her mouth, gripping it at the base, and lovingly slid her tongue up and down. Fargo's heart fluttered.

Her head bobbed up and down as she pleasured him with her mouth. Fargo groaned in ecstasy and let her have her way with him. He was eager to sample her goodies, and Sarah sensed it. She returned to him, and they embraced, kissing passionately. He eased her onto her back and settled himself on top of her. She wrapped her legs around him and ran her hands up and down his taut, muscled back.

He held her tightly, kissing her lips and nuzzling her neck. He found one firm, sweet nipple and sucked it deeply, giving it tiny little nips that made Sarah gasp in pleasure. He did the same to the other nipple, until he knew his lust could be contained no longer. Sarah eagerly spread her legs and gently guided him in. She wrapped her legs around him again, lifting up, as Fargo plunged his rod into her.

His thrusts were steady, and she trembled in her need for him. He slid his hands under her cheeks and continued his rhythmic thrusting. She rubbed her thighs against his legs and nibbled his ear. Her breathing quickened with his every stroke as he buried himself as deeply into her as nature allowed.

He pumped her harder as the intensity of their love-making grew. Her fingernails scraped his back, making him even crazier with unbridled lust.

"Oh, do it to me, you bad boy," Sarah moaned, but not loud enough to wake her aunt and uncle across the hall. "Oh, God, Skye . . ."

Fargo sucked her left nipple furiously, sliding his shaft in and out of her with total abandon. He knew he wouldn't be able to hold back much longer. Sarah climaxed with a high-pitched squeak in his ear and clutched him for dear life. Only moments later, Fargo exploded deep inside her.

They continued holding each other even after climax, catching their breath and basking in the bliss of pure carnal ecstasy. Then, Sarah asked him softly, "What are you thinking about, Skye?"

"I was just thinking about all the years I've wasted collecting stamps," he said.

She hit him on the leg. It had only been minutes since they'd finished, but Fargo was ready for another round of fun. It didn't hurt that Sarah had taken to diddling playfully with his manhood.

Fargo said, "I was wondering—"

"Why I sent Deke away so I could be with you?" she asked.

"That's about the size of it."

She said, "He's a good man, Deke is, and I wouldn't do anything in the world to hurt him. We're getting married next month, you know."

"So I heard tell," Fargo said.

"He'll make a good husband," Sarah said. "It's just that Deke's not . . . too exciting sometimes. He's a good deal older than me, so naturally a girl my age, well, has certain needs. You understand."

Indeed he did. He said, "Maybe you're just not ready to settle down yet, Sarah."

"Maybe," she said, "but at age twenty, in a town like Flatwater, I'll be an old maid on my next birthday. Makes a girl think."

"Makes a man think, too," Fargo said. "What you need are some sweet memories to get you over the kinds of rough spots you find in marriage."

"And I suppose you'll help me with those sweet memories?" she asked.

He would, and was now stiff enough to prove it. He said, "Let's live tonight like it's our last."

"It might be," Sarah said smiling slyly, "if Deke catches us."

Tucking that possibility neatly into the back of his mind, Fargo rolled her onto her belly and slid on top of her. He moved his hands under her luscious mounds and entered her from behind, and they went at it again at a slower pace this time. Fargo kissed the back of the neck and worked his way around to her mouth, where they kissed passionately. They couldn't get enough of each other, though they did their best for the next few hours.

25

They made love long into the night, until the dark sky showed signs of brightening.

"We better end this," she said. "It's almost time for Aunt Emma and Uncle Lars to get up. We have to open the café."

It was just as well. Fargo was exhausted. They'd done it three times already. Four, if one included when he fell asleep on top of her; Fargo didn't know if that one counted.

He got up and started dressing. He aimed to go to the one hotel in town and get himself a room, then do some serious sleeping. He was pulling on his boots when Sarah asked, "Will I see you again?"

"That's up to you," Fargo said.

"I don't think it is," Sarah said, "but don't worry, Skye. I'm marrying Deke Thornton, so there are no strings attached. What we did here tonight, and what we may do again, we're going to take to our coffins."

Fargo kissed her good-bye. He said, "I'll be around."

"I'll leave my window open," she said.

Fargo smiled and made his way out that very window. He started climbing down the tree, taking the branches slowly until he reached the ground. He dusted himself off and walked three steps—directly into Deke Thornton.

"Do you think there's anything that goes on in this town that I don't know about?" he asked Fargo. Thornton's face held no expression whatsoever.

Fargo never had time to answer, not that there was point in trying to explain it. Thornton's punch felt like a mule kick under Fargo's chin, the marshal putting his entire 220 pounds into it. Fargo's head snapped back like the cap on a bottle of a sarsaparilla, his eyes rolling up into his head.

2

Mace Tidley had been riding shotgun on the Holladay Overland Mail and Express Company ever since that old skinflint Ben Holladay had started up the stagecoach line a few years earlier. He'd ridden through blizzards in Colorado Territory, blistering heat in Kansas, twisters right here in Nebraska Territory, and even a plague of locusts in Montana Territory. One of those little ugly brown buggers had even ended up in his gullet, damn near choking him.

Mace Tidley was forty years old and made sixteen dollars a month for fighting the elements and whatever Indian tribe was stirring up trouble, so that the mail and the stagecoach passengers made it to their destinations with scalps intact. There hadn't been any serious Indian trouble since that murdering band of Sioux cut a wide swath up north two years back. Lately, except for the occasional ambitious stagecoach bushwhacker Tidley was only too happy to blast in the gut, things had been peaceful on the run from North Platte to Ogallala.

Beside him, Harlan Dundy snapped the reins twice. The horses snorted and made tracks. Sniffing the air, Dundy said, "Rain's a'comin'."

There wasn't a cloud in the sky, but Tidley knew from experience that it was a mistake to dismiss Dundy's predictions. The man could smell bad weather the way a fly could smell a buffalo chip.

"When do you think, Harlan?" Tidley asked.

Dundy's nostrils worked furiously. To a stranger, the man might have looked as if he'd been having a conniption fit. "Shouldn't be long. Within the hour, I'd reckon."

Tidley grunted. It was at least four hours to Flatwater. They were riding some harsh country now, with nary a tree in sight. A hard rain could land them waist high in mud.

They were carrying four passengers: a ruddy-faced banker type out of Grand Island named Chester Shottish, and a fallen dove named Carlotta Liddiflower Marcell who'd been run out of Gothenburg and was looking to ply her trade in a more hospitable environment. There was also an ugly old lady, Mrs. Arabella Hatley, who'd boarded in North Platte and complained about every bump. Next to her was a snake-oil salesman by the name of Samuel Pruett Drinkwater. He hadn't been run out of North Platte exactly, but neither was he invited to stay. His miracle elixir didn't kill anyone, but it did produce some nasty hangovers. Never one to overstay a welcome, Drinkwater moved on.

"Figure maybe we ought to hole up somewhere till the storm passes?" Tidley asked.

"Hole up where?" Dundy replied. "Ain't nothin' but dirt and rock for the next sixty miles less we head for the river. Might as well push on through."

On the horizon, Tidley could see the beginnings of storm clouds. The rain and lightning were bad enough. He hoped there wasn't a twister or two keeping them company.

Inside the stage, Drinkwater was sneaking nips from a medicine bottle, extolling the virtues of Drinkwater's Very Special Purplebark Miracle Elixir. He appeared to be his own best customer.

"A fine, fine concoction," Drinkwater was saying. "The recipe for which was passed down to me from my paternal grandfather, Pilkington Lovejoy Drinkwater, who sampled it from a friendly tribe of Mishagossi Indians nigh on forty years back. Afflicted he was, with a particularly virulent case of *canis delirious* while tramping the saw-grass territory we now know as Florida, following a skirmish with hostile Seminoles. Near death, Grandfather Pilkington was rescued by a beautiful young squaw named Smells Her Toes, who gave to him to drink the very same elixir you see right here."

Drinkwater polished off one medicine bottle and reached for the next, unscrewing the cap. Carlotta Marcel smiled politely at Drinkwater's half-cocked sales pitch. She wouldn't have minded a pull or two from his bottle of snake oil. Beside him, Mrs. Hatley refused to even look at him, trying instead to wedge herself into as tight a corner as the seat allowed.

Chester Shottish merely looked disgusted. He said to Drinkwater, "You, sir, are a silver-tongued liar. That poison you're hawking is nothing more than some cinnamon, sugar, allspice, and wood-grain alcohol. Why—"

"And how would you know that, sir?" Drinkwater interrupted. "Would you be one of my former customers?"

"I most certainly would not," Shottish huffed. "The very idea! Where I come from, we tar and feather your ilk and run them out like common prairie rats."

Drinkwater said, "I thought you looked familiar."

Outside, lightning illuminated the dusty prairie. It was followed by a deafening clap of thunder that made all four of the passengers jump slightly where they sat. The rain came not five minutes later, first in plump droplets, then in blinding sheets. The wind whipped up, and Dundy had a tough time keeping the team of horses on the straight and narrow.

"We best head closer to the river," Dundy yelled over the wind. "Ought to be a ridge where we can wait out this storm. This one's a corker, Mace. Ain't gonna let up no time soon."

Tidley agreed. As they approached the ridge—Dundy knew every inch of the territory along the North Platte—a violent bolt of lightning struck not ten yards away, spooking the horses. A clap of thunder followed. Tidley didn't notice the reins slip out of Dundy's hands; indeed, because of the hard rain, he didn't even realize that the left side of his face was covered with Dundy's blood.

Dundy turned slowly and looked at Tidley. "Mace . . ." he croaked, and Tidley had just enough time to see the gaping hole in his friend's neck; the bullet had entered an inch above the collarbone and exited right below his jaw.

Dundy pitched forward and tumbled off the seat, disappearing from view.

"Sweet Jesus!" Tidley cried, going for his rifle, but too late. Several shots rang out, and one of them found its target, taking Tidley in the meaty part of his left thigh. More shots came, from atop the ridge, more than likely, and two more hit home, slamming into Tidley's chest. Mortally wounded, he vainly tried to raise the rifle to return fire when half a dozen more shots pierced the air, one of them hitting Tidley squarely in the face. He fell backward off the stagecoach and was dead before he even hit the mud.

The horses, more spooked than ever, began running wild, rocking the coach violently. Mrs. Hatley went flying forward into Chester Shottish, her face landing squarely in his crotch. Carlotta Marcel started screaming bloody murder as Drinkwater was thrown hard against the door, his sample case and bottles flying everywhere.

The passengers were dimly aware of shots being fired outside, but in the confusion they had no way of knowing that the team of horses were systematically being slaughtered. As the last horse went down, the back left wheel of the carriage picked an inopportune time to strike a huge hunk of rock jutting out of the ground. The carriage, still moving but with nowhere to go, listed to the right, slamming the four passengers against the side. It tipped over and crashed into the mud, careening twenty yards before coming to a stop, the wheels still spinning.

Inside, there was shocked silence, then Mrs. Hatley started screaming. She was lying squarely atop Drinkwater, whose legs were sticking straight up at an angle that afforded him a look at his feet he hadn't seen since he was a baby. The crash had half sobered him. He pushed the fat old biddy off of him, then managed to kick the door open. He climbed up and peered out, getting a faceful of driving rain. What he saw finished the job of sobering him up completely.

Four men, sitting atop horses, were aiming very long rifles at him.

"Stand and deliver!" cried the man in the middle.

"I beg your pardon?" Drinkwater asked, blinking rain out of his eyes.

"Y'all come out of there, one at a time, and real slow like," the man said now, and from his tone, not to mention the size of his weapon, Drinkwater knew things weren't as they should be.

Below him, Shottish and the others were attempting to untangle themselves from each other. Drinkwater looked down at them and reported, "There appears to be some men out here . . ."

Shottish ignored him. He said, "What in God's name happened? Where is that blasted Mace Tidley? A fine state of affairs this is. A miracle we're not all dead."

Mrs. Hatley was whimpering, a long gash in her forehead leaking blood. She had struggled up to a sitting position on Shottish's lap. He angrily pushed her away, where she tumbled on top of Carlotta Marcell, whimpering even louder.

"Shut your pie hole, woman," Shottish snapped at her, "and get your foul carcass off me!"

The old girl got a little more hysterical. Carlotta Marcell tried to comfort her. "It's okay, Mrs. Hatley," she said. "We've just had a little accident." She then turned and angrily said to Shottish, "Why don't you go suck a lemon, mister?"

Mrs. Hatley calmed down a bit, until she realized who was supplying the comfort. She broke away from Carlotta and said, "I'll be fine, thank you very much."

Drinkwater said to the others, "Stay calm—I do believe we're being robbed. Just thought you'd like to know."

He climbed out of the overturned coach, then helped Carlotta Marcell and Mrs. Hatley out as well.

The rain was still pelting down in gushing sheets. Both women gasped audibly as they spotted the men on horseback. Even in the pouring rain, it was easy to see that the men were dirty, unshaven, and probably lacking in social skills. And undoubtedly deadly. Drinkwater shuddered.

Shottish made his way out of the coach, jumping to the ground, surprisingly nimble for a man of his girth. He straightened his necktie and slicked back what little hair he had left on his fleshy skull.

"Sue their asses off, that's what I aim to do, the minute we get to the next telegraph station," he groused. He glanced at the men with the rifles, did a double take, and then saw the dead horses. Assessing the damage, he looked sour and said to the men with the guns, "And how much is this going to cost me?"

The rider in the middle dismounted, ignoring Shottish's outburst. Clearly, he was the group's leader. "Get the cashbox," he said to his buddies, shoving his rifle into the scabbard and producing a pistol.

The two other riders dismounted and started rummaging through the heaps of cargo and luggage that were sprawled all around the overturned stagecoach. The bandit leader approached them slowly, as if he had all the time in the world.

"Surely you don't intend to rob us?" Shottish asked. "How far do you think—"

The leader was on Shottish in an instant, striking him in the nose with a balled fist. Shottish let out a pained howl and sagged to the ground, covering his wounded nose with his hand. Blood streamed through his fingers.

"Shut your face, old man," the bandit said as Shottish whined in pain. The leader paid him no mind. He stuck the barrel of the pistol under Mrs. Hatley's chin, then yanked off a very expensive-looking brooch pinned to her chest and said, "I'll be takin' this." He added, "I'll take the wedding ring, too, granny."

"Oh, no, please!" Mrs. Hatley cried. "It's of no value, I swear it. My late husband—"

The leader squeezed the trigger, not even blinking. The shot echoed through the rainy afternoon, and Drinkwater watched in numb horror as half of Mrs. Hatley's head turned into a thick red vapor, teeth and bone and brain splattering on the underside of the stagecoach.

Carlotta Marcell screamed, and Drinkwater screamed, too, though he wasn't aware of it. The leader jammed the barrel of the gun into Carlotta's mouth and said, "I think I want you to shuddup." She stopped screaming, tears mingling with the rainwater streaming down her cheeks.

The two men came scurrying over, carrying the cash box. "Here it is, Sherman," the first one said.

Sherman ignored them and grabbed the front of Carlotta's dress. In one neat swipe he ripped it right down the middle, taking her corset with it. Her milky-white breasts flopped out into the rain. Sherman started fondling them. He said, "Nice rack, lady. You look like a whore. You a whore?"

Carlotta, Drinkwater saw, had quickly regained her composure. She answered, "Yeah, I'm a whore, and if you were worth breaking my nails on, I'd rip your ugly face off."

Drinkwater closed his eyes, waiting for the shot to ring out, but none did. Instead, Sherman chuckled and said, "I bet you screw like a jackrabbit, don't you?"

"You'll never find out, you piece of dirt," Carlotta said, hate coating every syllable.

Sherman holstered his pistol. He grabbed Carlotta by the hair and started slapping her viciously. She took the punishment wordlessly, resigned to the stinging pain. This wasn't the first time she'd been backhanded by a man.

Drinkwater was scrambling toward them even before his brain registered the forward motion, and the words that came tumbling out of his mouth sounded a million miles away.

"She's just a woman, for pity's sake—" he started to say. Sherman spun toward him and slammed his palm against Drinkwater's chest, sending him stumbling backward into the mud. As Drinkwater lay there helplessly, Sherman drew his pistol and shot him in the left shoulder. Drinkwater cursed in pain and rolled into a little ball.

Enraged, Carlotta sprang out at Sherman like a rabid animal and grabbed his gun hand, sinking her teeth into it like a ravenous coyote. Sherman easily pushed her away. She went skidding into the mud.

His expression never changing from the placid, deadly mask he wore, Sherman said to her, "I likes 'em feisty. Don't go nowheres, honey."

On her hands and knees, Carlotta made her way over to Drinkwater and took him in her arms. His shoulder was a bloody hash.

"You damn crazy fool," she murmured.

Drinkwater's eyes fluttered open. His first vision was that of Carlotta's beautiful white mounds dangling an inch from his nose. He managed a weak smile.

He said to her, "I do believe I've annoyed that gentleman."

Carlotta snorted. "Some gentleman."

Sherman raised his pistol in the air and squeezed off a shot.

"Okay, Ma!" he hollered. "All's clear."

A brilliant bolt of lightning streaked across the sky, illuminating the banks of the Platte. Out of the rainy gloom emerged a passel of the meanest-looking men on God's green earth, nearly a dozen of them. Leading them was a short, stout, bantam little person in a large ten-gallon hat who immediately started barking out orders to the others, some of who scattered and started picking through the spoils.

"Everything gooden, son?" the short person asked.

Sherman said, gesturing over at Drinkwater and Carlotta, "They won't be no trouble, Ma."

It took a moment or two for Carlotta and Drinkwater to realize that the short person was actually a *woman*—a squatty, mammoth-breasted behemoth with bad teeth and uglier than sin, but a woman nonetheless, dressed like a man. A jagged scar decorated a face that was plenty bad to begin with, running from under her left eye down below her chin, giving her puss a sinister, lopsided look. She could have been forty, she could have been older; it was difficult to tell, what with the wide-brimmed hat she wore.

"Sherman . . . Ma . . ." Drinkwater muttered. "Dear God, no!" He'd spent enough time in jails across the territory, and had seen enough wanted posters, to realize what they were up against.

"It's the Purdy gang," he said weakly, blood oozing from his bullet wound. "This isn't going to be pleasant for either of us, dear."

Carlotta's eyes widened in terror. Everyone from Texas to Montana knew about the Purdy gang. Ma

Purdy had five or six sons, a killer brood who were the spawn of the devil himself.

Ma whipped out a pistol and shot open the cash box.

"Sherm, get at it," she barked to one of her sons. Sherm Purdy fell to his knees and started rummaging through it. There were some bills and bags of silver. Sherman counted quickly.

"Fifty-three dollars and about twenty more in coin," he grunted.

"That all?" Ma asked, and she didn't sound happy. "Seventy dollars?"

"Shit," said a slightly taller, stockier, version of Sherm Purdy. "Hardly seems worth the effort, Ma."

"Shut yer craw, Coffin," Ma Purdy snapped.

"I told you we should've headed south instead of west," Coffin Purdy complained. "If you'da listened to me—"

Ma silenced her son with a backhanded fist to his Adam's apple. Coffin grabbed his throat and started making gurgling sounds, then dropped to all fours gasping for breath.

"Shouldn't oughta talk back to Ma," chastised a runty, weasel-faced youth. "Serves you right."

"You shut up, too, Digger, or you'll get some of the like," Ma said. The youth fell silent and started brooding.

Four of the gang had already noticed Carlotta, who'd managed to cover herself up somewhat. She was still cradling Drinkwater in her lap. They came over and stood above them. Two of them had scruffy, tobacco-stained beards; the third was missing most of his left ear and right eye, which was a hollow socket he didn't bother to conceal with a patch. The fourth man was a walleyed, drooling moron, with spiky red hair and an idiot grin.

"You be comin' with us, girly girl," the one-eyed man said, grabbing Carlotta by the arm. "We got plans fer y'all." He said to one of the brown beards, "Ain't she a tasty one, Asa?"

"A warthog'd look tasty to you, Hardsock," Asa said. He grabbed Carlotta's other arm and together they dragged her to her feet.

"Gimme some sugar, girly girl," Hardsock said, and forced his lips against Carlotta's. She sank her teeth into his lower lip and tasted blood. Hardsock howled and pushed her away. She slammed into Asa, who spun her around and threw his arms around her from behind in a bear hug. The others cackled in glee at the little show, loving it.

"You got some fire in you, Lady," he said. He grabbed her titties and gave them a healthy squeeze.

Carlotta responded by yanking out a four-inch hairpin—Drinkwater never did see from where—and jamming it into Asa's arm.

He bellowed in rage, and grabbed her by the throat, the pin still firmly embedded in his meaty arm, and hurled her against the overturned coach. Carlotta hit face first and was knocked out cold.

Hardsock, clenching a bowie knife in his fist, started to go to her, saying, "I'm gonna carve that bitch a new face."

Asa grabbed Hardsock by the arm and said, "You ain't a-gonna do squat till we've had our fun with her, unnerstand?"

"You can unnerstand this!" Hardsock lashed at Asa's face with the knife and deftly severed a chunk of the bearded man's nose. Everyone laughed louder, enraging Asa even more. He drew his pistol and was about to kill his erstwhile friend when Ma fired a shot that kicked up dust at Asa's feet.

"Shut up, you ignorant piss doodles," she ordered, "or I'll kill you both!"

Asa was holding his bloodied nose. "Little shit bird cut me," he protested.

"He touched me," Hardsock said to Ma. "You know I don't like bein' touched."

"Way you smell, Jonah," Ma countered. "I wouldn't worry on it too much."

"You promised, Mother Purdy," Asa complained. "When we found a woman, you said we could have at her. Didn't she promise, Jonah?"

"Damn right," Hardsock agreed, their animosity already forgotten. "You shore did, Mother."

"Shut up, both y'all," Ma said. "Be time for that later. We still got some work to do." She walked over to where Shottish was quivering beside the coach. Dried blood covered his suit.

"What's your name, Mister Man?" Ma asked him, resting the barrel of her pistol squarely between his busy eyebrows.

"S-S-Shottish," he stammered. "Chester Shottish."

"I hear tell, Mr. Chester Shottish," Ma said, "that sometimes the stage company chooses to hide their money wads somewhere other than in the cash box. You heard this also?"

"I don't think . . . I mean, I've never . . . I don't know," Shottish stammered, his face whiter than new cheese.

"He don't know," Ma Purdy said to the gang. "Ain't that something?"

"Leave him to me, Ma," Digger Purdy said. "I'll teach him what fer."

Ma Purdy ignored him. Digger, Ma's youngest, set to brooding again. Nothing he did was ever right with her, and that hurt. While Coffin Ike recovered from Ma's punishment, Sherman enjoyed watching his beloved Ma griddle this well-dressed fat man from town. The others in the gang stood and watched as well, transfixed by this little old lady who could strike terror into the heart of a man twice her size.

Even in the chilly rain, Shottish was sweating like a pig. Ma Purdy said, "Knowed a lotta men, Chester Shottish, and one thing don't ever change—they lie through their lousy teeth damn near ever' chance they get."

Shottish opened his mouth to reply, then thought the better of it.

"Yep," Mother Purdy said. "Men are pond scum, born liars one an' all."

She pumped two bullets into Shottish's left kneecap, nearly severing the leg below it. Shottish fell to the muddy ground and screamed, and who could blame him?

"Where's the goddamn money, you lyin' sack of shit?" Ma asked.

Shottish writhed in agony and cried out, "There's . . . there's no money. There's nothing."

"This is the first of Octember," Ma Purdy said, "an' I hear-tell that the first of ever' month is payday for your stagecoach employees. I hear tell there ought to be a king's ransom somewhere on this fancy wagon."

Ma pumped two more bullets an inch or two from Shottish's head, sending mud flying into his eyes. "Talk to me, fat man, or I'll blow yer butt off."

"Nothing," Shottish said. "Not a penny."

Ma shot him again. Shottish flopped in the mire like a tadpole.

"Under the forward seat, the money is there," Shottish said. His face was waxy, and he was still sweating. "Three thousand dollars in payroll."

Sherman and his brother Coffin Ike were already there, climbing into the overturned stagecoach. The sound of ripping boards was heard, then Sherman's head bobbed up like prairie hen's. He proudly held up a big black valise, then heaved it in Ma's general direction.

Ma shot off the pathetic little lock on the bag, then kicked it over to Digger, her baby boy, "Count it, sonny," she said.

Glad for her attention, Digger emptied the bag, and bundles of bills flopped out. He looked up at Ma, and smiled. "Money is good," he said.

"Damn right," Ma said, then turned to Shottish and said, "I told you not to lie to Mother Purdy."

"I didn't," Shottish pleaded. "I swear I didn't."

"Lyin' scum," Ma said, aiming her pistol at his head.

"No, please," Shottish said. "I have children, and a wife."

"Got kids my ownself. You got my sympathies, Chester," Ma said, and pumped two bullets into his brain. Shottish's body jerked violently, then went still. Two of the gang, Strap McClure and Micah Gorr, set onto his corpse and started going through his pockets.

Ma turned to Sherman and said, "Men lie."

"If you say so, Ma," Sherman said. He pointed to Carlotta, who was just coming around. "What about her?"

"We'll keep her fer tonight, make the boys happy," Ma said. "But just for tonight. Too much pokin' makes a man's brain soft. In the mornin', kill her, that is if the boys don't fuck her to death first."

"Sure thing, Ma," Sherman said.

"An' keep yer brothers away from her—yer own-self, too," Ma said. "You share her with them lowlifes, no tellin' what kinda disease you'll catch."

"Okay," Sherm said. "Ma, I was thinkin'. Now as we've got some money, you reckon we ought to head out to Oregon Territory like we planned?"

"We'll go, son," Ma said. "But I got us some plans first."

"We're pretty hot, Ma," Sherman said. "Got some heavy law breathin' down our backs."

Her oldest son's opinion couldn't have mattered less to Ma Purdy. She said, "We'll pitch camp here for the night. This territory's sweeter than molasses pie. Lotta small towns in this territory, rich farmers and ranchers with nice fat boodle bags full of green—and there ain't no one can stop the Purdy gang when they get their blood up."

Sherman said, "Ma, I think we'd be wise to head north whilst we can. Winter's a'comin', and the going'll be plenty harsh."

Ma looked at her oldest son, her angry gaze burning right through Sherman's skull. She said to him evenly, "You do what I say."

Sherman knew all too well the price for disobeying his mother. He gave her a cold smile and went to do her bidding.

The rest of the gang had found Drinkwater's traveling case full of seventy-proof snake oil and were guzzling it down. Strap McClure and Micah Gorr tried to sneak past Mother Purdy with the booty from the bodies of Shottish and Mrs. Hatley, consisting of cash and jewelry and a pocket watch McClure took a special shine to.

Ma turned to them and said, "Where you goin',

boys?" She took off her hat. McClure and Gorr meekly dropped the goods into it. "The watch too, Strap," Ma said.

McClure, looking sulky, pulled it out of his pocket. He said, "Never miss a dang trick, do you?"

"No," Ma replied, "and you best be grateful I don't." As McClure started to drop the expensive watch into Ma's hat, she thought for a moment, then said, "Oh, go ahead and keep it. Won't hurt to have someone around here knows what time it be."

Most of the boys, already pretty liquored up on Drinkwater's elixir, dragged Carlotta Marcell, kicking and screaming, back to the horses, where she was slung over Asa Miner's saddle.

"Go easier with her, boys," Ma cautioned, "iffen you aim to get the best of what she's got."

One by one, the members of the Purdy gang saddled up and headed back to camp. As always, Ma was the last to leave the scene of their crimes. She walked up to Drinkwater, pulling out her pistol.

Ma said to him casually, as though discussing the weather, "Kids, try an' figger 'em. Either they don't do as they're told, and even when they do, they cock it all up to hell an' back." She asked Drinkwater, "You got any kids?"

"None that I know of," Drinkwater said.

"Been a bastard of a day." She checked the barrel of her pistol, counting bullets. "You ever have one of them rotten days?"

"I think I'm having one now," Drinkwater replied.

Ma shot him once in the chest. Drinkwater seemed to rise up, then fell on his side, rolling facedown in the muck. Ma holstered her gun and went to fetch her horse. "Yup," she said. "Been a real bastard of a day."

"Who's her?" Lila Mae Purdy said, looking all wrathy, hands defiantly on hips. Lila Mae was seventeen, the only girl child of Ma Purdy's murderous brood. Unlike Ma, who had a face like a bucket of manure, Lila had a sweet little baby face, a head full of curls, and proud, perky tits, a real sweet package. At least, that was the opinion of the non-Purdy factions of the gang—not that Ma would let any of them near her. Still, Lila Mae liked to whip the boys into a hot tizzy, wiggling her butt or shaking her luscious melons, then watch them fight over her.

Lila Mae hated competition of any kind, so she was less than thrilled as she watched Asa Miner pulling Carlotta down off his horse.

"Some whore, what's it to ye?" Asa wanted to know. "Your ma said we could keep her."

"Shit," Lila Mae snorted, grabbing some of Carlotta's hair and yanking her head back. "She ain't even pretty."

Carlotta, barely conscious as Miner held her up, spit in Lila Mae's face. Lila would have ended it right there with the knife she toted in the back pocket of her overalls, had Miner not whisked her away. "Yeah, but she's got lots of spunk," he said.

Lila Mae saw one of the gang, Bill Dill, dismounting. He was a hard case out of Oklahoma Territory, as most of them were. He'd been riding with the Purdys since Lila Mae was just a pup. She knew Dill was sweet on her. For her part, Lila Mae considered him the most desirable out of a very undesirable gaggle of prairie scum and murderous half-wits. She stated her willingness—on more than one occasion—that she'd happily surrender her virginity to him. Bill Dill valued his life more than any chance at Lila Mae, however, knowing full well that Ma and her brothers would separate him from his balls if he so much as looked at her crooked. Not that the old battle-ax ever let Lila Mae out of her sight long enough to accomplish much.

Lila strolled slowly over to him and rubbed up against him. "How many folks you boys kill today, Billy?" she asked.

"I dunno," Dill said, tying his horse down. "Four or so."

"Did they bleed lots?"

"Yeah, they bled some," Dill said.

"Did *you* kill any of 'em, Billy?" Lila Mae asked, getting a little excited.

"One of the stage drivers, I think," he answered.

"Them's that got killed, did they scream like they was in pain?" Lila Mae asked now.

"Yeah, some," Dill said, adding, "You ought not to ask questions like that, Lila Mae. Ain't healthy."

"I was thinking, Billy," Lila Mae said, stroking his arm. "Let's you an' me run off to New Orleans. I could get money. I know all Ma's hiding places. Soon as we're shut of Ma and the rest, you can have your way with me as much as you want."

"Your ma wouldn't like that," Dill said.

Lila Mae said contemptuously, "You're just afeared of Ma, that's what I think."

He turned to her. She *was* pretty, and it was hard to believe, once again, a beast like Mother Purdy could have spawned such a lovely little creature. Lila Mae had hit a sore spot, though, and he said, "I ain't afeared of no one, not your ma nor your brothers."

Lila Mae smiled. "That's right, Billy, you ain't afeared. And I'm tired of sleeping on the ground and eating slop. You and me, Billy, we could light out and be rid of Ma and my stinky brothers. Tonight, Billy. Let's leave tonight."

Ma and the brothers Purdy rode up just then. Lila Mae said to Dill, "We best break this up. Maybe I'll come and visit with you later."

Ma surveyed the cook fire and the kettle of beans simmering over it. Ma was pleased that Lila Mae had found enough dry wood for a fire. She had some fine plans for her little Lila Mae, Ma did. Marry her off to one of them Seattle millionaires, maybe, or set her up with a high-class whorehouse.

"That supper best be ready, girl," Ma hollered at her daughter, "or I'll wail the tar outta you. Where's Lumbert?"

"Over by the fire, Ma," Lila Mae said. There, poking a big stick into the embers, was her half-wit brother, Lumbert. He was a year younger than her, cross-eyed and dumber than dirt, with the brain of a flea. He didn't do much but drool and shit, and Lila Mae was weary of minding him while Ma and the boys rode off and had all the fun.

Another of the gang, a deadly half-breed named Cherokee Sam, who never said a word and seemed to lurk only in shadows, had been left behind to watch over Lila Mae and Lumbert. Cherokee Sam came and went like a phantom, but it was a given he was never far away. He'd been with Mother Purdy and her boys since the beginning, ten years ago back in Missouri, when they were cutting their criminally insane teeth on murderous raids on small farms and towns, slaughtering everything in their path.

Asa Miner, Jonah Hardsock, and the others had taken Carlotta off somewhere and her screams began in earnest. They stripped her bare naked; since Asa had lugged her back to camp, it was only fair he got the first crack at her. He dropped his pants and fell on her, grunting and sweating.

"Give it to her good, Asa," Strap McClure squealed happily, egging him on. The other boys chimed in with their own witty comments and observations.

Jonah Hardsock cried out, "Ain't you a-gonna milk her, boy?"

"Yeah, suck her dry, Asa!" Micah Gorr said. "What I wouldn't give to have them titties filled with tequila."

Asa Miner, struggling to locate the whore's jelly roll without success and getting increasingly frustrated, growled, "You mind? A man likes privacy when he's bein' tender with a lady."

"Tender?" Hardsock asked. "You're lucky she don't barf in yer ugly face."

Carlotta was too weak to protest much, pathetically pummeling her fists on Miner's thick head. He finally found what he was looking for, though with some effort, and had his pleasure. When he was done, Strap McClure, who'd won a coin toss to be next, took his turn. Hardsock and Micah Gorr waited eagerly, ignoring the enticing aroma of beans wafting in their direction. Bill Dill wanted none of it, and concentrated instead on trying to find a dry spot to sleep on, toting his bedroll as far away from the raping scum as he could. They all made him sick.

He wondered if Lila Mae would come to him tonight.

Ma and her sons set down to devour the beans. Digger pushed his brother Lumbert out of the way and slopped a pound of beans into a bowl. Lumbert started blubbering and slinging snot all over his dinner. Coffin Ike, on the other side of him, rapped Lumbert hard on the head a few times. Lumbert shut up immediately, and stuck a finger up his nose.

"Leave the boy be," Ma snapped at Ike as she slurped down some beans. "Lumbert ain't right, you know that."

"Lumbert got rocks in his head," Digger said, and started giggling. Ike giggled, too.

Ma said, "Shut your ignorant faces, both of y'all."

Ike griped to his sister, "These goddamn beans taste moldy—"

Lila Mae, in a pissy mood, reached into the bubbling pot of beans with the ladle, and flung them into her brother's face.

"But good," Ike added quickly.

Lila Mae leaned over the simmering pot and filled a plate for herself. Ma caught Digger sneaking a peek at Lila Mae's bosom bobbing invitingly in her tight undershirt. The look on Digger's face smacked of more than just brotherly love.

Ma laughed and hit Digger upside the head. She said, "I knows what on yer mind, boy, but don't even think on it. Lila Mae's way too good fer her own kin."

"What's next, Ma? We headin' north?" Ike asked.

Ma said, "Not on your kidney plaster. There's riches to be found right in this here Nebraska Territory. Which are the closest towns to the north and west?" This she asked Sherman.

Sherman consulted a crudely rendered map he usually toted in his saddlebags, but kept handy now, already knowing Ma's intentions. He studied the map for a moment, then answered, "Beaver City is a two-day ride to the north. Weasel Creek is due west, a three-day ride. And there's a spot, maybe half a day to the northwest, could have promise."

"Yeah?" Ma asked, sounding interested now. "What's it called?"

"Flatwater," Sherman said.

"Anything there worth takin'?" Ma asked.

"Could be," Sherman said. "I hear tell it's a fair-size town. Might even be a bank. But I still think we should make for Oregon Territory like we planned, put plenty of distance between us and the law."

"Yeah," Ike chimed in. "You said we wuz going to Oregon, Ma. I wanna go to Oregon."

"Me, too, Ma," Digger whined.

"Shut your pie holes," Ma barked. "Ain't no law we can't handle our ownselves. We're goin' all right, but when I'm damn good and ready. I ain't gettin' any younger, and I aim to get as much as I can so's I can retire an' spend my days smokin' my pipe and sittin' by the fireplace. If that means hittin' a few towns along the way, so be it. And you needle dicks are a-gonna help me."

There was no dissent in the ranks until Sherman said, "We start takin' on whole towns agin, a lotta the boys over there are likely to get theyselves killed."

"That's the idee, son," Ma cackled. "After this, who needs 'em? We'll get to the Territory faster without 'em. Less money to split, too."

Sherman grinned, and so did Ike and Digger. They cottoned to the notion instantly.

Ma said, "Digger, tomorrow at sunup, you and Lila Mae take yourselves a ride into this Flatwater. Act like yer just passin' through. See what's there, if it's worth raiding or not. An' see what they got in the way of the law, what kind of firepower they got. We'll head north up to the South Loop River country an' meet up with y'all there day after tomorrow."

"Okay, Ma," Digger said. "I can do that."

Ma turned to Lila Mae and said, "And keep him out of trouble, girl. In quick, out quick, then hightail it out."

"Why do I have to go, Ma?" Lila Mae complained. "Digger smells so bad I start swoonin' when I'm downwind of him."

"Shut yer filthy mouth, bitch," Digger snapped, spraying bean juice.

"Because I said so, that's why," Ma said.

The discussion was over. They all went back to their beans. Some distance away, they could hear Carlotta's tormented moans and the men already fighting over who was next.

Ma said, "I wouldn't trade places with that gal for all the corn likker in Missoura."

Some time later, Bill Dill tossed fitfully in his bedroll, not quite asleep and not quite awake. He felt something flutter pleasantly against his groin. He opened his eyes, and felt hot breath in his ear.

"Don't say a word, sweetheart," Lila Mae whispered. She had her hand in his pants and was fondling his pecker. He was as big as a barn and twice as hard.

Lila Mae unbuttoned her shirt and exposed her firm, well-rounded breasts to him. "Taste me, Bill honey," she said. "Now."

Dill surrendered to his lust and jammed his face into her chest, kissing and licking her womanly charms. "Do you like it, Bill honey?" Lila Mae asked, running her fingers through his hair. "Do you wanna put it in me? I'll let you, Billy, if you want. Do you?"

Dill gasped, saying he did. She massaged his throbbing manhood, bringing him to the brink of climax. As his passion mounted to the boiling point, Lila Mae pushed him away and said, "Then take me away from them, Bill. Just the three of us—you and me and Ma's money. Say you'll do it, Billy, and you can have at me."

There was no getting around it; he wanted her more than he'd ever wanted anything. He said, all out of breath in his excitement, "Okay, Lila Mae. Anything you want, darlin'."

"Here's the plan," Lila Mae said. "I'm gonna tell you where Ma keeps her money."

She told him, and quickly ran down what they would do the day after tomorrow. Bill Dill agreed, saying, "anything you want, darlin'." In his condition, Bill Dill would have agreed to French kiss his horse. Lila Mae's hand slithered up and down his shaft, knowing he was ready to erupt. "Understand, Billy? You be there, okay? With the money."

"Yes," Bill Dill moaned and pleaded, "Finish me off, Lila Mae . . . please, girl."

"Finish yourself," Lila Mae whispered, and was gone like a phantom, drifting away into the gloom of night. "And think of me whilst you're doing it."

"Shit on fire." Bill Dill gripped his pecker and tried to do just that. His sweetmeats unfortunately had other ideas, and all his love juices flowed backward in a painful rush. There would be one teeth-gritting case of blue balls to contend with shortly. He got up from the bedroll and ambled into the woods to relieve some of the pain.

"Some kid," he muttered, unaware that less than eight feet away, Cherokee Sam silently faded into the night as well.

3

Fargo was making passionate love to Sarah Lundegard in an open field full of daisies and wildflowers and sweet-smelling grass.

Sarah had her legs wrapped around his buttocks and was nibbling tantalizingly on his left ear. He was sliding his throbbing rod in and out of her. Sarah's hot breath on his neck only served to make him hotter.

"Love me, Skye darling," she gasped underneath him, her nipples erect against his chest. "Love me forever, Skye!"

They rolled around in the dew-covered grass until Sarah was on top of him. He started thrusting up into her, grabbing her firm bottom and burying himself inside of her.

He was nearing his climax when it suddenly started raining—not dainty raindrops, but a downpour of biblical proportions. His eyes opened, and the rain ended as quickly as it had started. Sarah Lundegard was gone, and in her place, Fargo realized with some alarm, was the old geezer Mushy Callahan, he of the old saddle and empty belly. Mushy was holding an empty water bucket over Fargo; the last few drops trickled out and landed on Fargo's chin.

Fargo was soaking wet, and he was clutching a filthy pillow.

"You in the habit of screwin' even whilst you're asleep?" Mushy asked.

"You in the habit of pouring water on people for no damn reason?" Fargo asked, wanting to throttle the old buzzard. His head hurt too much, though, to even contemplate movement of any kind.

"Marshal said fer me to wake you up," Mushy said. "Marshal says you slept enough."

"How long have I been out?" Fargo asked.

"Few hours," Mushy said. "Judgin' by that there dream you wuz having, I'd say not a minute too soon. Ain't never seen a man humpin' a pillow before."

"No," Fargo said. "I reckon your kind usually prefers farm animals. Would it be safe to assume I'm in jail?"

"Brother, are you ever," Mushy replied.

Fargo recalled hitting Thornton's fist with the left side of his face. Then he noticed the dried blood on his shirt. He felt his nose and winced at the pain.

"What are you doing in here?" Fargo asked Mushy.

Mushy said, "Hell's bells, Fargo. I'm the town character and a drunk besides. It's my sworn duty to raise hell. Got me a snootful last night and tried to crap in the graveyard. Old Deke was awful mad at me. But not as mad as he is at you. Gossip is, Deke Thornton's got it in fer you, Skye Fargo, and the whole town knows why. Something to do with Sarah Lundegard, they're sayin'."

Small towns, small minds, Fargo thought angrily. He should have known better than to poke the fiancée of the town marshal. Still, Sarah had supplied him with enough pleasant memories to last a long, long time.

The door to the jailhouse flew open, and Fargo was relieved to see not Deke Thornton—whom Fargo was in no mood to deal with now—but a short, somewhat squat and chunky man with a close-cropped black beard. He wore wire-framed spectacles that sat low on the tip of his nose, and a bowler hat. He was carrying a carpetbag and looked generally harried.

"Mornin', Jacob," Mushy said.

"And a good morning to you, Mr. Callahan," the man said. "How's the pain in your noggin? The bicarbonate of soda helped maybe?"

"Greatest hangover cure known to man, thank you," Mushy replied. "But I suspect Fargo's head hurts worse." He pointed to Fargo, who was looking a little green around the gills.

The man said, "Ah, yes, so this is the patient? A chair would be nice, Mr. Callahan. And the cleanest water you can find, please." Mushy lugged a wooden chair into the cell and the bearded man sat.

The man said, "I'm Jacob Belinsky, Mr. Fargo. I run the dry goods store here in Flatwater."

"Jacob is one of the Jewish tribe they got in New York. Ain't never takes his hat off," Mushy explained. "Started doctorin' up when our sawbones, old Ezra Phipps, passed on last year. Studied it back East, he did."

"For one year at City College in New York, that's all," Belinsky said. "A person shouldn't get excited."

"Jacob's bein' modest," Mushy said. "He can slice a corn offen your toe or deliver a baby with the best of 'em."

"I don't need a doc," Fargo said.

"You'll forgive me, sir, but I think you do," Belinsky said, and gently felt Fargo's face with the tips of his fingers. Shaking his head in sympathy, he said, "Oy! Quite a shiner you're going to have there. And

54

from what I hear, you had it coming. So tell a person, where does it hurt?"

"Everywhere," Fargo said.

"It's a start," Belinsky said, rummaging through the carpetbag and pulling out iodine, cotton, and bandages.

"Do I look as bad as I feel?" Fargo asked.

"You shouldn't know," Belinsky said. He dabbed the gash above Fargo's cheek with iodine. "So you're Skye Fargo, the one everyone is kibitzing about?"

"That would be me," Fargo said.

"They say you kill people, Mr. Fargo," Belinsky said as Mushy delivered the clean water. "From this you make a living?"

"Sometimes," Fargo said.

"Only in America," Belinsky said shaking his head disapprovingly. He dipped a clean towel into the water and started cleaning Fargo's damaged face. "So the rumor around town is, you and our Miss Sarah Lundegard have become, you'll pardon the expression, biblical together."

"Is that a fact?" Fargo said.

"Where there's smoke, there's salmon," Belinsky said. "A rumor is as good as the truth, if people choose to believe it, Mr. Fargo."

"Could be you're right, mister," Fargo said.

"So, did you *shtupp* her?" Belinsky asked.

"If *shtupp*ing is what I think it is, it's none of your business," Fargo said.

"I'm not asking for business," Belinsky said. "I'm asking because our Mr. Thornton planned to marry Miss Sarah, and the good people of Flatwater very much like the man and wanted the wedding to happen. You've upset God's plan, Mr. Fargo, and that's not a goodness."

"Sorry," was all Fargo could offer.

"Then again," Belinsky said, "if the foot was on the other shoe, what man wouldn't take pleasure from Miss Sarah if it was graciously offered?"

"Then you understand," Fargo said.

"I'd be a complete schmuck if I didn't," Belinsky said.

Belinsky wanted to bandage Fargo's face, but Fargo refused, saying, "Best not. Bandages make a man look weak."

"You're expecting trouble maybe?" Belinsky asked.

"What do you think?"

"I think you've already got trouble," Belinsky said, and cleaned out the last of the small cuts on Fargo's face, then stepped back to admire his handiwork. "Done. In a few days, you should pardon the expression, you'll be in the pink." He started packing up the carpetbag.

Fargo reached into his pocket and said, "How much do I owe you, mister?"

Belinsky said, "Keep your money. If you're a smart man—and I have every reason to believe you are—you'll use it to get as far away from Flatwater as your long legs will carry you."

Thornton finally appeared, coming into the jailhouse. He moved slowly, looking a little tired. He nodded at Belinsky. "Jacob."

"Good morning, Deke," Belinsky said.

"All finished here, Jacob?" Thornton asked.

"I was just leaving," he said, and quickly made for the door.

Thornton looked at Mushy and said, "Didn't you tell Norval Stoon you'd shovel out the stables for him today?"

"I reckon I did," Mushy said and followed Belinsky out the door.

Thornton sat on the chair opposite Fargo's bunk. He was silent for a minute or so, his gaze fixed on Fargo. Then he said, slowly and evenly, "Do you know why you're still alive? Do you know why I didn't gut you with a dull butter knife and leave you out in the sun for the buzzards?"

"Look, Thornton," Fargo said. "I—"

Thornton held up a hand to silence Fargo. He said, "Killing you would have been too quick, Fargo, too painless. You're not getting off that easy."

Fargo opened his mouth to respond, but Thornton cut him off again. "Don't say anything, Fargo, because there's nothing you can say that's gonna save your dumb ass."

"Thornton, if you want—"

"What I want," Thornton said, "is for you to get the hell out of my town. But there's something you got to do first."

"And what would that be?" Fargo asked.

"You're gonna marry Sarah," Thornton said.

"I am?"

Thornton nodded. "I don't see any way around it," he said. "If you don't make an honest woman outta her, it makes me look very bad to the town folk. My reputation in the territory wouldn't be worth a plugged nickel. Then I would have to kill you."

"A shotgun wedding?" Fargo said. "I don't rightly think so, friend."

Thornton stood and drew his Colt, pointing it at Fargo's head. "Then you die now."

"That's murder, pure and simple, Thornton," Fargo

said, little doubt in his mind that Thornton was in a sour enough mood to make good on his promise.

"I've studied the law," Thornton said. "Of course it's murder!"

"Wouldn't be fitting for a man of the law to kill an unarmed person," Fargo said.

Thornton cocked the trigger. "No, it wouldn't," he agreed, "but it sure would feel good. So I'll ask you again: You gonna marry her or not?"

"No," Fargo said. "And you can't make me."

"Then say some prayers, if you ever bothered to learn any."

Fargo refused to believe it would end here, getting shot by a jealous man. "I ain't a religious man, but I will perhaps say a few words," he said, and dropped to his knees. Suddenly, he then hurled himself at Thornton, ramming his fists into the man's belly. Thornton stumbled backward, sending the gun flying. Fargo raised up and landed one on Thornton's chin for good measure. This time, Thornton didn't even flinch. He lashed out with a left hook and popped Fargo on the cheek. Fargo got mad and moved in for the kill, swinging his fists like a windmill. Trouble was, Thornton blocked every punch Fargo threw and came back with a couple of his own. He outweighed Fargo by twenty pounds at least and was two inches taller, but Fargo had tangled with worse. Thornton moved to deliver a punishing right cross when Fargo popped him as hard as he could in the jaw. Thornton was stunned momentarily, and Fargo expected him to drop.

The tough bastard didn't, though, and rebounded fast enough to grab Fargo's neck and dig his fingers into Fargo's windpipe. Fargo tried to suck in air and jammed his thumbs into Thornton's eyes. The two men tumbled to the floor and rolled around, gouging eyes and squeezing throats.

It was then that Sarah Lundegard chose to pay a visit. She was carrying a glass of milk on a tray. She took three steps inside just as Fargo and Thornton rolled in her direction, bumping into her. She fell forward, the glass and tray flying across the room, and tumbled over both of them.

Fargo and Thornton were oblivious to her presence, still grappling and pummeling each other. Sarah grabbed the tray and started smashing them over their heads with it.

"Stop it now, you chunkheads!" she bellowed as the fighters tried to shield themselves from the blows.

"Damn it all, Sarah," Thornton said. "We got unfinished business."

"He's right," Fargo said. "You better go now, honey."

"Don't you tell her nothing," Thornton said indignantly. "I'll tell her when to stay or leave. She's still my fiancée."

"Yeah, but I'm the one who has to marry her," Fargo protested.

"And don't be callin' her honey, neither," Thornton said with some heat. They started tussling again.

"Who's marrying who around here?" Sarah wanted to know.

Thornton said, "You're marrying Fargo here today, at three o'clock. That's the way it's got to be."

"Is that so?" Sarah asked.

"You're gonna marry him," Thornton said, "and then you're gonna leave town with him. I don't want to see either of you until the day I die. Come to think of it, I don't want to see you afterwards, neither."

"What if I don't want to marry him?" Sarah said,

her face getting red. "You ever think of that? And maybe I don't want to leave town."

"You'll never know a day's happiness," Thornton said to her. "You know the people in this town, Sarah. You'll be a fallen woman in their narrow little eyes. Is that the kind of life you want for yourself?"

"I was unfaithful to you, Deke, not the town," Sarah said. "Let's not pretend otherwise."

"Who's pretending?" Thornton asked.

"You don't want to marry me?" Fargo asked, sounding a little hurt.

Sarah turned to Fargo. "Do you want to marry me?" she asked skeptically.

Fargo took his time, choosing his words carefully. "Well," he said, "you're a very pretty gal, Sarah, and if I ever decided to take myself a wife, then I suppose I could do worse— "

"There," Sarah said to Thornton. "He doesn't want to marry me any more than I want to marry him. Am I safe in my assumption, Skye Fargo?"

Sarah didn't wait for his answer, for which Fargo was grateful. She said to Thornton, "Don't punish Fargo for what happened last night, Deke. Put the blame on me, if it helps matters any." She took off her engagement ring and grabbed Thornton's hand, dropping it in his palm.

"Sarah . . ." Thornton said, looking confused, but no more so than Fargo.

"I'm not asking you to forgive me, Deke," Sarah said heatedly. "But let's get one thing clear: I'll marry *whom* I want to marry, *when* I want to marry him. And I'll be damned if any man, sober or stewed, will dictate otherwise. And to hell with anyone in this town who chooses to judge me. Are we all on the same page here?"

Fargo and Thornton both nodded.

"Fine," Sarah said. "Good day to you both."

With that, Sarah left, slamming the door behind her.

"That's quite a gal you got yourself there, Thornton," Fargo said.

Thornton looked at Fargo, disgusted. He said, "I got me some business, Fargo. If you know what's healthy, you'll be long gone when I get back."

"What about my money?" Fargo asked.

"It's here," Thornton said. "The bank in Salinas wired it early this mornin'. Go see Henry Twerk over to the Flatwater Bank. He's holdin' it for you. Collect your blood money, Fargo, and get the hell out."

Thornton jammed his hat onto his head and headed out. No sooner did the door close than Mushy Callahan reappeared, carrying a tray.

"You wantin' any breakfast?" Mushy asked. "Got it from the café."

In spite of everything, Fargo was ravenous. He lifted the napkin off the plate. On top of the scrambled eggs was a note from Sarah, which read: "Will I see you tonight?"

Fargo tucked the napkin into his shirt and dug into the eggs with a smile on his face.

"Don't go pushin' your luck any further, Fargo," Mushy said, reading Fargo's mind. "If it was me had Deke Thornton angry, I'd be out of town faster than a roadrunner in a tailwind."

All things considered, the old geezer was probably right. But oh, that Sarah Lundegard. . . .

"Don't give Deke any more grief, Fargo," Mushy said. "He's got problems. The evening stage from North Platte never arrived yesterday. Deke's worried."

"Indians?" Fargo asked.

"Could be," Mushy said. "Were some talk about a raiding party up around Ash Hollow, but that's nigh on a hundred miles to the north. Don't seem right, somehow."

No, it didn't. There hadn't been any serious Indian problems, or so he'd heard, in a month of Sundays. "When was the stage due in?" Fargo asked.

"It was the six o'clock stage," Mushy said, "which usually gets here promptly at eight."

Fargo tried not to care. It was trouble at the very least; at the worst, the Almighty only knew. Fargo was tired. He wanted his money. He wanted a drink. More than anything, he wanted to hightail it out of Flatwater. The town proved to be more trouble than it was worth. Except for Sarah Lundegard. The gal had gotten under his skin and no mistake.

What was a man to do?

Fargo was two or three miles out of Flatwater before he began to relax. The Ovaro was rested and ready; the stable had done an excellent job. He was in no hurry, but neither did he dawdle. He was tired, but it was exhilarating to be on the move again. As for Sarah Lundegard, well, their paths would cross again if the Fates willed it.

Fargo was heading east—the same direction as Thornton, most likely. He figured on maybe heading back to Kansas. There was a Chinese restaurant in Dodge City he liked. Or maybe St. Louis. He'd always done well, ladywise, in St. Louis.

Collecting his money from the bank had been as easy as pie. Henry Twerk, a short, portly, balding man, had tried to convince Fargo to leave the cash in his bank, spinning some wild promises about the future of Nebraska Territory and all the opportunities the country presented to a young man such as Skye Fargo. Twerk had declared, "Why, the corn grows halfway to heaven, and with some good cattle, and a fine woman by your side . . ."

Fargo had declined with gracious thanks. He was not a man to let grass grow under his feet. He'd gotten his money and was on his way to whatever the future held. No telling what that was, but the not knowing was the part he liked best.

In the distance, Fargo saw turkey buzzards circling. He felt a knot in his gut. He crested the top of a ridge and saw the overturned stagecoach. Fargo's day decided to get worse. The knot in his gut grew tighter. He touched the spurs to the Ovaro's flanks and off he went.

The buzzards were already feasting on the bloated carcasses of a man and a woman. Fargo dismounted and fired a couple of shots into the air and the scavengers took to the skies. It was already clear that the dead woman had been shot at close range—too close for it to be anything but a cold-blooded execution. The dead man, too, had been shot, but at a slightly greater distance. This was no Indian attack.

Fargo heard a moan. He turned, already clearing leather. He saw another man, fifty yards off, writhing in pain and gamely trying to swat flies off of himself. Fargo grabbed his canteen from the Ovaro and made his way over to the poor bastard. He hunkered down and poured some water onto the man's lips. Fargo saw two bullet holes. Singly they wouldn't have been fatal; together was another story. The man had lost a lot of blood. Too much.

Fargo poured water onto his neckerchief and dabbed it on the man's forehead.

"More water," the man croaked. "Please."

"Sorry, no can do," Fargo said. "Not with them bullet holes in you. What in the hell happened here?"

The man tried to swallow without success. "The girl . . . go see to the girl," he croaked.

Fargo poured more water on the man's lips. He said, "Forget it, friend. She's layin' over yonder with most of her head gone."

"Not that one," the man said, every word a pained effort. "Miss . . . Marcell. They took her over there . . ." He tried to point in the direction of the river.

Fargo went to check into it. Judging from the generous amount of footprints—and those of their horses, he estimated at least ten men had taken a part in this massacre. He came upon their old camp without trying. A tired tendril of smoke rose from the ashes of a cook fire. The night had been cool; the fire had been kept going until an hour before sunup.

It was then that Fargo spotted Deke Thornton, squatted on his haunches maybe fifty yards away, his back to Fargo.

"Thornton?" Fargo said.

He received no response, and made his way over there. Thornton had his head down, idly running dirt through his fingers. Not far away lay the nude corpse of what had once been a pretty lady. She'd been shot straight through the heart, right where she lay more than likely. Her lifeless face was twisted into a mask of agony and terror, as though she'd seen the Devil himself.

Fargo's belly did some back flips as he hunkered down next to Thornton.

"I hate to think of what they did to her," Thornton said.

"Sometimes it's best not to," Fargo replied.

"I guess you already figured it weren't Injuns," Thornton said.

Fargo nodded. "We got a survivor over there. Best we tend to him till we get this sorted out."

Thornton looked at him and said, "I ain't asking for your help, Fargo."

Fargo rose and said, "Fine. Then let's get these poor souls buried and I'll be on my way. I reckon the driver and the shotgun rider are dead somewheres, too. We best get to it."

They both grabbed shovels and started digging. The job went faster as both men put their backs to the task, and soon Carlotta Marcell, Chester Shottish, and Mrs. Arabella Hatley were planted safely in the ground. When they were done, Thornton said, "Maybe we should say some words for their souls."

"So say 'em," Fargo said, and walked back to see to Drinkwater, who was swimming in and out of consciousness.

"What's your name?" Fargo asked him.

"Drinkwater," the man said with some effort. "The girl . . ."

"She's dead," Fargo said. He rummaged through his saddlebags for something to bandage the man with. He pulled out some cotton and a bottle of whiskey. He cleaned Drinkwater's wounds as best he could, then managed to stop the bleeding. Thornton had joined them by now. He asked, "Will he make it?"

"He will if we get him back to town and pick that lead out of him," Fargo said.

"Who did this to you?" Thornton said to Drinkwater.

Drinkwater grimaced in pain, and he said, "Ugly old lady . . . they called her . . . Mother."

"What did you say?" Fargo asked.

"Mother . . . Purdy," Drinkwater gasped.

Fargo's blood went cold. Thornton's face turned white.

"Most unpleasant woman," Drinkwater managed to say.

"The Purdy gang is here?" Fargo asked.

"It can't be," Thornton said, his voice cracking. "It just ain't possible. Last I heard, they was massacred by the militia outside Houston."

"No," Fargo said. "You got it backwards. They massacred the militia."

"Will they come to Flatwater?" Thornton asked. There was no trace of animosity toward the Trailsman now, only fear of what was to come.

"They might," Fargo said. "They just might."

"Did they say where they were going?" Thornton asked Drinkwater, who sank into unconsciousness again. Thornton slapped the salesman's face, not hard, but enough to rouse him momentarily. "Where did they say they were going? Dammit, tell me, mister!"

"Didn't discuss . . . travel plans with me," Drinkwater said, and went out again.

"Shit," Thornton said, and made for his horse. "Then we best get ready. We need this man alive, Fargo, to get some hard answers for some hard questions. I'll ride on ahead. Can you get him back?" Without waiting for an answer, he mounted and rode off.

Fargo set about making a pallet to haul Drinkwater back to town with. He grumbled, "I always get the lousy jobs."

"We all do, sir," Drinkwater said weakly.

4

Flaterwater may have been a hick town in the middle of nowhere, but Fargo had to admire the way they all swung into action the moment he dragged poor Mr. Drinkwater into town. The good citizens moved quickly, and within minutes Drinkwater was on a bed in the back of the Belinsky's mercantile. Sarah and her aunt Emma were lugging boiling water over from the café. Her uncle Lars brought some whiskey and clean towels. Mushy went off to fetch the mayor and the others on the town council. An emergency meeting was needed, Thornton claimed.

Fargo stuck around. He and Sarah tried not to look at each other, and Thornton tried not to stare at Fargo and Sarah.

Jacob Belinsky, preparing the patient, ripped Drinkwater's blood-soaked shirt down the middle, saying admiringly, "Nice material."

"Is he gonna make it, Jacob?" Thornton wanted to know.

Belinsky answered, "You're in my light, Marshal."

Thornton hastily stepped away from the window.

Belinsky examined the bullet holes. "Such a badness, grown men shooting with guns," he said disdainfully.

"Them bullets will have to come out," Fargo said.

"So you thought I was maybe planning to leave them in?" Belinsky asked.

Belinsky went through his medical bag and pulled out some alcohol rub. "You'll be kind enough to hand me a clean towel, Lars," he said.

"A towel, ya, Jacob," Lundegard replied, and handed it to Belinsky. "He is going to be well?"

"From your mouth to God's ear," Belinsky replied, and set about cleansing the wounds. He examined the damage. "Two holes where there shouldn't be any, and thank God they didn't hit him in the *kishkies.* Does this man have a name?"

"Drinkwater," Fargo said. "Samuel Pruett Drinkwater. I do believe he's a snake-oil drummer, judging by all the empty bottles scattered all over creation. Our friend here fairly reeked of it."

"Drinking up his profits," Belinsky said. "Not good business, but it may have saved his life."

Belinsky pulled some surgical gadgets out from his bag and poured alcohol over them. He bent over Drinkwater and started to operate.

"I hope you know what you're doing, Jacob," Fargo said.

Belinsky said, "*You're* still here, aren't you?"

"Jacob knows exactly what he's doing, dear," Sarah said to Fargo, grabbing his arm to shut him up.

"What do you mean calling him *dear*?" Thornton shot at Sarah.

"I can call him anything I want, dammit," Sarah spat back.

"Hush, Sarah!" her uncle Lars said. "By yimminy, saying such a word."

"You hush, Lars," Emma snapped back at her husband. "Don't interfere."

"Oy *gevalt,* everybody hush," Belinsky said irritably. "This isn't a cheesecake I'm working on here! I think

68

you should all kindly leave and let me save Mr. Drinkwater in peace, thank you. Emma, I would be eternally grateful if you could maybe bring me a nice pot of tea. This may take some time."

"Tea, ya," Emma said, and scurried out. "Right away, Jacob."

"You always burn it, Mama," Lars said, following her out. "I vill make the tea for Jacob."

Once they were gone, Sarah asked, "So do one of you want to tell this poor little lady what the hell is going on around here?"

"I think you best go, Sarah," Thornton said. "Trouble may be coming."

"He's right, Sarah," Fargo said. "Big trouble."

"I just told her," Thornton said irritably to Fargo. "You ain't got to repeat it."

"I wasn't repeating anything," Fargo said sharply. "A man can talk if he's of a mind to."

"And you talk even when you're not," Thornton snapped.

Fargo wasn't sure what Thornton meant by that exactly, so a comeback was difficult. Mushy Callahan saved him the trouble, barreling into the store breathlessly, wheezing and sweating despite the chill in the air. He looked like he'd just seen a ghost.

"This is bad, Deke," Mushy said, still trying to catch his breath. "A real pickle, yes indeedy. I need a drink, Lord, do I need one. Jacob usually keeps a bottle around here for snakebite . . ."

Mushy started rummaging through the shelves, looking under bolts of cloth and boxes of all kinds of stuff. Thornton said, "I thought I told you to fetch the mayor and the others."

Mushy ignored him, continuing his search. "Must

69

have whiskey," he muttered. "Must have whiskey . . ." He was soon successful, uncorking a bottle of bourbon he'd found stashed under a pile of petticoats.

Before he could drink, Thornton snatched the bottle away and asked, "Talk first, drink later."

"Was one of the Purdys," Mushy said. "Digger, I think, though he's growed some since I last seen him."

"Where was he?" Fargo asked.

"Over to the Hanged Dawg," Mushy said. "Was some gal with him. A looker, too. Not more'n sixteen, seventeen."

The Purdy gang, here?" Sarah asked incredulously. She started to tremble. "Oh, dear God . . ."

Fargo said to Thornton, "A scouting party would be my guess."

Mushy took the bottle from Thornton and started drinking. Thornton said, "Sarah, maybe you and your kin best pack some stuff and head on out till we got us a better idea of what's to be."

"Might be better if they stay put," Fargo said. "We don't know where the Purdys are holed up."

"Yeah," Thornton said by way of agreement. "We best make some plans without panicking the whole town. We need to round up every gun in the county, and quick. I'll put the word out, and—"

"Wait a minute," Fargo said and grabbed the bottle from Mushy.

"What the hell you think yer doing, you pecker-wood?" Mushy asked indignantly.

"Tell me that part again," Fargo said to him. "About Digger Purdy growing up."

"Sure as shit has," Mushy said. "He weren't no bigger than a sprig when I last laid eyes on him."

"And when was that?" Fargo wanted to know.

"Ten years back," Mushy said. "When I was ridin' with Ma Purdy and her boys."

"We need to have us a little palaver," Fargo said to him.

"Joined up with Ma Purdy back in eighteen and forty-something, don't recollect exactly," Mushy said. "Was younger then, and full of vinegar. Had us a roost up to Weatherford, in the Oklahoma Territory. We stole ever'thing what wasn't nailed down tight. Must've been twenty, twenty-five of us back then. Some real mean bastards. Puts my teeth on edge just to think about it."

What teeth? Fargo wanted to ask, but didn't.

"Had her a passle of boys, Mother Purdy did, and all by different daddies. The bastard sons of the worst kinda white-trash savages God saw fit to give life. Seemed like Mother was taking a new husband ever' week. But then agin, most of us boys got to know Mother in the biblical sense. It was what you call 're-quired duty.' And the less said about that, the better. Tweren't so bad if you drank lots of whiskey first. Hell, I knowed men who'd screw a goat." He nodded at Sarah. "Beggin' your pardon, ma'am."

"A goat?" Belinsky asked from across the room, where he was working on Drinkwater. "Such a thing is possible?"

"Sure, why not?" Mushy asked. He drank, then said, "That gal with Digger—he's Ma's favorite, I re-call—I do believe that's Lila Mae, Ma's only daughter. Been ten years, and she was a just a rug rat then, but that's her. Probably just as crazy as the rest. Ain't nearly as many now with Mother, or so's I've heered."

"The Texas Rangers thinned their ranks pretty good in Waco," Fargo commented. "Two years ago. It was a nasty fight. But the Purdys got away and vanished into the dust."

Mushy took sips from the bottle, enjoying such a rapt audience. By this time, the mayor, Henry Twerk, and the men of the town council, such as it was, had arrived. Twerk also owned the Flatwater Bank, so of course had opinions on everything. Dud Kissel owned the Shady Rest Hotel, and usually deferred to Twerk on most matters. Alvin Platt operated the bakery and several other businesses, and tended to defer to Kissel. And Norval Stoon, who owned the Hanged Dawg and the stable, didn't much give a rat's ass just as long as business was good.

They were all crammed into Belinsky's store. Belinsky had finished removing the lead from the snake-oil salesman—Drinkwater would live, but he wouldn't be dancing anytime soon.

"We need to talk to him," Fargo told Belinsky.

"I don't think that's a good idea," Belinsky said. "He's very weak. He needs to sleep now."

"I'm sorry, Mr. Belinsky," Fargo said, "but there's some questions only he can answer."

Drinkwater was dozing peacefully. Some color was creeping back into his complexion. Fargo gently shook him until the salesman awakened, with much difficulty.

"Drinkwater," Fargo said. "Can you hear me?"

Drinkwater managed a painful nod. Fargo asked him, "I need you to remember, friend—how many were there that did this to you?"

"So tired," Drinkwater said wearily. "Please . . . let me sleep."

"Sleep later," Fargo said. "Tell me—how many were there?"

"Horrid people," Drinkwater croaked. "Drank all my stock."

Drinkwater started to fade. Fargo shook him awake again. "How many, Mr. Drinkwater?"

"Rats in the corncrib," Drinkwater said deliriously. "No more tar and feathers, dear people. Must get stage to St. Louis. Must—"

"He's half out of his mind," Thornton said. "You'll get nothing out of him, Fargo."

"We've got to," Fargo said, then asked Drinkwater, "How many Purdys were there?"

"Counted . . . about ten," Drinkwater remembered now. His words came out slowly, painfully. "Did I mention . . . they were . . . most ill-mannered? Not . . . nice at all . . . Yes, about ten. Crude, foul-smelling scoundrels, all of them."

"I think he's talked enough for one day," Belinsky said now, and pushed Fargo gently out of the way. "Leave him in peace, Mr. Fargo, and let him get better."

"Ten," Fargo said. "Sounds about right. Rangers shot down thirteen, fourteen of them I remember reading. That' leaves ten, give or take. A small army. And they'll tear this town apart."

"I ain't a bad person, you understand," Mushy continued, "Thievin' was just another way to fill my belly. Runs in the family, I reckon. My daddy was a horse thief back in Indiana. They hung him. But I ain't never kilt nobody, if that's what y'all are wonderin', 'cept some Sioux Injuns, and they had it comin', the murderin' devils."

Mushy took a long pull of whiskey, and started smiling as he remembered. "Had me surrounded on a hillside up to Medicine Bow, they did, fifty braves if there were one. Filthy redskins. Johnson and me, we . . . did I ever tell y'all about Liver Eatin' Johnson? Used to rip out Injun livers and have 'em for breakfast, he did. One time—"

"Get to the meat of the matter, old man," Fargo snapped, reaching for the bottle.

"I'm gittin' to it," Mushy whined, and jerked the bottle away from Fargo's reach. "Like I said, there ain't nothing the Purdy clan likes better than killin'. I once saw, was in Missoura, old Mother Purdy kill a man in cold blood. A storekeeper in Poplar Bluffs, name of Elwell. Ma slit him from neck to nuts, cackling like a hen whilst his guts spilled all over the floor. Her boys laughed, too, even Digger, who weren't more than eight or nine at the time. Then they killed the poor bastard's daughter, too, when she wouldn't stop screaming. Had their way with her first, you can be sure. Young gal, I remember, cuter than a bug's ear.

"Lit out the next day, I did," Mushy said. "Robbing is one thing—I suspect I'll have plenty to answer to when my time comes—but killin' was where I always drew the line. The spawn of the devil, that's what they are. Ma Purdy and her boys, they'll cut your throat then go have a dinner of beans and bacon. There's some darker stuff about them, too, but bein' as there's a lady present"—he motioned toward Sarah—"I'll say no more."

"All these years," Belinsky said. "Why hasn't God seen fit to strike them dead?

"She's a cagey one, Ma Purdy is," Mushy said. "Just when the law thinks they're in one place, they pop up in another, cuttin' a swath of pain an' misery. Now the Purdys are here, in your town, and it'll take an army to stop them."

"Nearest troops are hundreds of miles away, at Fort Hastings," Fargo said. "Never get here in time, even if we could get word."

"So we're on our own," Thornton said.

"That's about the size of it." Fargo said.

"Thornton," Henry Twerk said, "I hold you responsible for this devastating dilemma. If you were doing the job you were hired for—"

Fargo cut in, "He's doing the job he was hired for, Twerk, and if he wasn't, you'd be as good as dead—"

"Shut up, Fargo," Thornton said. "I don't need you to defend me." He ripped the badge off his vest and held it out to Henry Twerk and said, "The very moment you want this back, just say the word." He looked over at Sarah. "I got nothing keepin' me here anymore."

"Now, let's not be hasty, Thornton," Twerk said, wiping his sweaty brow with a hanky. "This is no time to get emotional."

"But what are we gonna do?" Norval Stoon asked. "Purdy and that lady are drinkin' in my saloon even as we speak."

"Not anymore they ain't," Fargo said. They all looked out the window. Digger and Lila Mae were strolling down Main Street. Digger was walking with a swagger, as if Flatwater were his and his alone. They headed into the café.

"Oh, my God!" Sarah cried and tried to rush out.

Fargo grabbed her as she was halfway out the door. "Not so fast, little lady," he said. "You just stay put."

"But my aunt and uncle are in there—they might need help," Sarah protested.

"I got another idea," Fargo said.

Mushy, temporarily forgotten, was sitting atop a crate of canned peaches and getting thoroughly soused. Fargo said to him, "So you're pretty familiar with the Purdy gang, huh?"

"Mister," Mushy said, "I know them real well, and there ain't a lot to like. But I reckon I know 'em as well as anyone who rode with 'em and lived to tell about it."

"Fine," Fargo said. "Then you're gonna mosey on over to the café and have a talk with Digger Purdy."

"Do I hafta?" Mushy asked.

"Oh yeah, you hafta," Fargo said.

"Don't kill Digger," Fargo said to Thornton as they half dragged a very reluctant Mushy Callahan across the street to the café. "We need him alive."

"I suppose you got a plan," Thornton said.

"Maybe," Fargo said.

"Gonna tell me what it is so I can hate it?"

"Sure," Fargo said. "Mr. Callahan here goes in the front. You and me go through the back door and get Sarah's relations out, then wait and see what develops."

"Why do I have to talk to him?" Mushy wanted to know. "Digger'd just as soon shoot me as say good mornin'."

"Make small talk," Fargo said. "Ask him about Ma—you know, how pretty she is these days, how's her health? Where's the gang camped, how many are there, stuff like that."

"What if he shoots me?" Mushy asked.

"We'll try not to let that happen," Fargo replied.

They left Mushy at the door, with instructions to get on inside. Fargo and Thornton ran around to the back of the café and slipped inside the kitchen quiet as mice. Emma was furiously frying up a couple of beefsteaks and weeping, on the verge of hysterics. Inside the café was the reason. Fargo could hear Digger Purdy screaming at Lars, who was hurrying toward them with a tray full of food. He set it down on the table and started off-loading dishes of bread and beans and coffee. There was a bottle of whiskey on the table.

"Move your bony ass, ya old fart," Digger bellowed. He was roaring drunk, it was clear, and hankering for trouble.

Lars was clearly terrified, so much so that he spilled water all over the table and, unfortunately, on Digger's lap. Digger jumped up and grabbed Lars by the collar.

"You stupid bastard," Digger said, and forced Lars facedown into a plate of steaming beans. "Spill water on me, will ya?" He lifted Lars out of the beans and shoved him. Lars pinwheeled backward and he crashed into a table.

"Papa!" Emma wailed, and Thornton put his hand around her mouth and hustled her out the back door.

Lila Mae giggled as Lars struggled painfully to stand up.

Digger said to her, "Shut your hole, Lila Mae." He drew his pistol and cocked it, fully intending to kill Lars. Fargo went for his gun; this wasn't what he had in mind at all.

Not a moment too soon, Mushy made his entrance.

"Digger Purdy?" he cried, stumbling over to the table. "Well I'll be damned to purgatory if that ain't you."

Digger turned to look at the man who was ruining his fun. Mushy grinned from ear to ear. He said, "It's me, Mushy Callahan. Used to ride with Ma and the boys, don't you remember?"

Digger didn't, not at first, but then most things took a while to sink into his pea-sized brain. He appraised Mushy with cold, hard eyes. "And is that Lila Mae I see here?" Mushy went on. "You weren't no bigger than a kitten last time I seen you. Growed up into a right pretty girl, you did."

"Don't ah knows you?" Digger drawled slowly. Lars was forgotten for the moment. "Ain't yer name Mushy?"

"Been tryin' to tell you, Digger," Mushy said. "Mushy Callahan. Used to cook for you and your brothers."

"Used to cook for us, didn't you?" Digger asked.

"Uh . . . how's Ma these days?" Mushy asked, running out of conversation quicker than he'd planned. Lars had wisely retreated to the relative safety of the kitchen, where Thornton summarily hustled him out the door.

"Y'all lit out on us," Digger said. "I recollect Ma talkin' about it, how she was a-gonna blast you a new butt hole if'n she ever seen you again."

"I didn't light out, Digger," Mushy said, sweating like a pig. Where the hell was Fargo, for the love of Jesus? "Never did such. Went out to get some supplies . . . and when I come back the next mornin', you was all gone."

"He's lyin', Digger," Lila Mae said. "You gonna let him lie to you, brother? Ma woulda kilt him by now. Or you just a gutless little puke?"

"You shut yer stinkin' mouth," Digger growled at her.

"Weren't like that at all, Lila Mae," Mushy pleaded. "Swear on a stack of Bibles."

"Nobody runs out on the Purdys," Digger said. "Think I'm a-gonna have to kill you."

"Do it," Lila Mae said, urging him on. "Make him bleed, Digger."

Mushy started backing up toward the door. "Now, Digger," he stammered, trying not to trip on anything.

"It's me, Mushy, your old pal. Ain't no need to kill an old friend."

"Maybe not," Digger said, following Mushy toward the door, until Mushy backed into a table. "But yer so damn ugly, I think I'll kill you anyway."

"I . . . we . . . Digger," Mushy said, stumbling over his words. "You don't . . . sweet Jesus, please—"

Fargo chose to burst through the Dutch door to the kitchen at that very moment, wearing a silly apron and carrying a tray. "Got some chicken-fried steaks here," he cried out and slapped the tray down onto the table and off-loaded the plates. The steaks were steaming hot and smelled mighty good. Digger forgot about killing Mushy and sat back down, tearing into the steak. Lila Mae likewise attacked her meal with gusto.

"Good," Digger said, swallowing the beef after only a couple of chews.

Lila Mae chose not to comment, devouring her steak. Fargo waited until they'd each swallowed twice, then slammed the metal tray against the left side of Digger's head, knocking him out of his chair. The energetic little desperado managed to draw his pistol and fire at Fargo before he hit the floor. The bullet went wild, missing Fargo by a foot. Fargo heard a roaring sound, doubtless Thornton discharging his rifle in their direction—and not caring too much what he hit, Fargo realized grimly.

Fargo ignored Thornton's shots and kicked Digger in the chin with everything he had. He actually heard Digger's thick skull knock against the wooden floor. Digger mercifully stayed down.

From the corner of his eye, Fargo saw Lila Mae whip out a knife. Before he could blink, he felt the blade sink into his left buttock cheek. Thornton, bless him, rushed up behind her and clocked her on the noggin with the butt of his rifle. She dropped like a sack of potatoes.

Fargo and Thornton both stood silently for a moment, letting it all sink in and catching their breath. Fargo said, "Little hellcat, ain't she?" He tried to reach the knife, which was nicely embedded in his flesh.

"First time I ever struck a woman," Thornton said.

"You picked a good time to start," Fargo said.

Fargo was still struggling with the knife. "Leave it be for me, Fargo. I been through this before," Mushy said.

"I bet you have," Fargo said.

Mushy yanked out the knife. Fargo made a sound somewhere between a grunt and a howl. Blood leaked from Fargo's wound.

Mushy said, "Gonna need you some stitches."

"Get Jacob over here, and pick up a bottle of whiskey," Thornton ordered Mushy.

"Dang blamed Purdy bastards," Mushy growled, running out. "Told you to let me handle them!"

"What do we do with our guests now?" Thornton asked Fargo.

Fargo sat down gingerly on the chair and said, "Throw this piece of slime into your jail. Leave the girl here. I'll tend to her my own way."

"You ain't gonna kill her in my town, Fargo, if that's what you're fixin' to do," Thornton said.

"Nothing as sloppy as that," Fargo said. "I'm aiming to let her go."

"Ever since you came to this town, Mr. Fargo, I've had more business than I can handle," Belinsky said, stitching up Fargo's wound. Fargo was bent over a table, his pants around his ankles. Lila Mae hadn't stuck the blade in too deep, fortunately. "You're a lucky man my father was a tailor, he should rest in peace. He could thread a needle in the dark and sew up a cuff so sharp you could cut your pinky on it. So tell me, how does a man get a knife in his *tuchas*?"

Fargo took long pulls off the whiskey bottle, each mouthful getting sufficiently larger with each ply of Belinsky's needle. Half the whiskey was gone, but the pain was still agonizing. Fargo helped himself to another long swig.

"Such craziness, a little girl like that with a knife," Belinsky said. He looked over at Lila Mae. Fargo had tied her into a chair, sparing no inch of rope. A trickle of blood from the wound in her head had dried on her face. She was still unconscious, but that wouldn't last long. Thornton and Mushy, meanwhile, had dragged Digger Purdy back to the jailhouse.

"Only in America," Belinsky said. "With the guns, with the knives, with the killing. Such a young girl she is!"

"Some folks are born evil," Fargo said, "some folks become evil, and some folks have evil thrust upon them. Little Lila Mae here, she got the best of all three."

Flatwater was in something of an uproar. Thornton was bombarded with questions from the townsfolk. They wanted to know what the hell was going on. Thornton wouldn't be able to keep the harsh truth from them much longer. Sarah had been pressed into action to quell some of their fears and to try to keep a lid on the Purdy powder keg.

"So what happens now?" Belinsky asked, stitching the last of Fargo's slightly embarrassing wound.

"You finish with me," Fargo said, "and then I have a little chat with our friend here."

Lila Mae started groaning, coming around. Belinsky

hastily completed his stitching. "You best leave now, Jacob. I want this to be a private chat 'twixt me and her," Fargo said.

"Remember, Mr. Fargo," Belinsky said. "A little kindness goes a long way."

Fargo looked over at Lila Mae, who less than ten minutes earlier had been more than willing to shove that knife through his gut and give it a hefty twist.

"I'll keep that in mind," Fargo said, and when Belinsky was gone, he grabbed a pitcher of cold water and dumped it neatly on Lila Mae's head. She sputtered back to consciousness and tried immediately to lurch out at Fargo, not realizing at first that she was trussed up like a Thanksgiving turkey. She wiggled and squirmed to get free, but wasn't going anywhere.

"Who the hell are you?" Lila Mae asked. Her face was all scrunched up in anger, but damn if she still wasn't pretty. A different brand of loveliness than Sarah—Lila Mae was pretty in a hardscrabble sort of way. Sensuality rolled off of her like a Galveston fog. With Sarah, it was there, but it didn't just jump out at a man.

"Who I am don't matter," Fargo said. "Who *you* are, well, that's something else. Ain't that right, Lila Mae?"

"How'd you know my name?"

"Everybody knows you, Miss Purdy," Fargo said. "Just like everyone knows your crazy mama. Where is she?"

"Like I'd ever tell you," Lila Mae said, and spat on Fargo's boot.

"You will if you don't want to see your fool brother hang before sundown," Fargo said, ignoring the slight for now.

"Go ahead and hang him, see if I give a hoot," Lila Mae said.

"Ma wouldn't like it too much," Fargo said.

Lila Mae thought about that for a minute. Then she said, "What're you aimin' to hang Digger for?"

"Seems your brother killed a man," Fargo said.

"He's always killin' 'em," Lila Mae said. "So what?"

"Well," Fargo said, "we tend to frown on such things around here."

"Gonna hang me, too, big man?" Lila Mae asked.

So much for Digger's fate, Fargo thought grimly. There was doubtless little love lost among the Purdy siblings.

"Ain't decided yet."

Lila Mae didn't miss a beat. With a huge, seductive smile, puffing out her breasts as best she could under the circumstances, she said, "Like what you see, mister?"

In fact, he did. His hesitation spoke volumes. Lila Mae moved right on in, saying, "I can be real friendly when I want to be."

"When you're not jabbing folks in the ass with that pigsticker of yours," Fargo said.

"That was before I knowed you," Lila Mae said. "Take me right here, big man, any way you want."

Fargo started untying her. Lila Mae threw off the ropes and bounded to her feet like a jackrabbit. She threw her arms around Fargo and kissed him hard on the mouth. She did taste sweet, like honey and pepper.

"You're a pretty one, you are," Lila Mae said, and immediately dropped her hand down to his crotch and gently squeezed his manhood. To his consternation, he started getting hard. Not wise, not in the least. This fetching young thing was lethal and no mistake.

She whispered, "Do what you will to me, and who's to know?"

"I would," Fargo said, pushing her away. "You don't have to love me to win your freedom, girl. You can go anytime you aim to. Your horse is waitin' outside."

"Why you being so kind to me?" Lila Mae wanted to know.

"I want you to go back to your ma," Fargo said. "Tell her we're fixing to keep Digger here for a day or two, just in case she's planning to ride on into Flatwater and make life unpleasant for everybody. You tell your ma, if I see one hair on her ass, we'll stretch Digger's neck like warm taffy."

"I'll tell her," Lila Mae said. "But she ain't a-gonna like it. You don't know Mother Purdy."

"No, I've been lucky till now," Fargo said.

"If she thinks Digger's in trouble, there won't be no stopping her," Lila Mae said. "She'll charge in here crazier than a shit-house rat madder 'n hell."

Fargo nodded and said, "We'll be ready, make no mistake."

Lila Mae made her way to the door while the going was good. She asked Fargo, "You aimin' to follow me?"

"No," Fargo lied.

"The hell you say," Lila Mae replied. "Follow me if you want, big man, but I ain't a-goin' back to Ma and the boys. I got me other plans."

Her horse was tied to the hitching post outside the café. Fargo escorted her outside and watched as she mounted up, saying, "Seeing how I'm letting you go, I figure I got the right to ask you a very important question."

"And what would that be?" Lila Mae asked.

"Your ma planning on cutting a swatch through this town?"

"More'n likely," Lila Mae answered. "She'll come lookin' for me an' Digger when we don't show up."

She jerked the horse's reins and said to Fargo, "Take care, big man. You ever get down to New Orleans, be sure and look me up."

"Maybe I'll do that," Fargo said, and watched as she galloped out of town. Thornton came up behind him and commented, "I still think it's a mistake lettin' her go."

"We ain't exactly letting her go," Fargo said. "She's going to lead us back to Ma and her bunch. Claims she ain't going back to her ma and the rest, and maybe she ain't. Then again, maybe she is."

"She'll know she's bein' followed," Thornton said.

"Yeah, she probably will," Fargo said. "Now, let's go see what Digger has to say for his ownself."

"He won't talk," Thornton said.

"Maybe he will," Fargo said. "I got an idea."

"I was afraid of that," Thornton said as they walked back to the jail.

"We'll need Mushy's help," Fargo said, looking at a gnarly old oak tree behind the jail. "Tell him to get some rope and fetch Digger's roan from the stable."

"I guess we can do that," Thornton said.

"Also," Fargo said. "Has Hiram Crimp been buried yet?"

"Don't believe so," Thornton said. "But I doubt he's in any position to help us now."

"You never know," Fargo said. "Maybe he is."

"This one's gonna be a pip, ain't it?" Thornton said.

Fargo replied, "Yeah, I suspect it will."

5

Digger was still out cold, bound to the rusty cot inside the jail cell.

Thornton gave him a good drenching with a pail of cold water—probably the closest Digger had come to clean water in years.

Digger stirred, then came awake.

As instructed, the town undertaker, Melvin Snoddy, had delivered the body of Hiram Crimp, late of the Armstrong Anvil Company, over to the jail, where it was now covered with a white sheet near the door. Snoddy had done his job well, but Hiram Crimp was still getting a little ripe. He had yet to be planted in Flatwater's Boot Hill, pending a decision on where to send the body, and Snoddy was loathe to have to dig him up at a later date—too expensive. As it was, he'd made nothing for his trouble. Billing the town took years.

Digger saw Thornton standing over him and tried to lunge at him. Digger didn't get far and succeeded only in spraining his wrist.

"What fer you got me tied up?" Digger asked indignantly.

"Because you're a murderer, that's why," Thornton said.

"I didn't kill no one," Digger protested.

"I'm afraid you did," Fargo said, lifting the sheet off Hiram Crimp.

Digger peered at Crimp's corpse. He said, "I ain't never seen him afore."

"He was walking into the café when you started shooting up the place," Thornton said. "Took him right between the eyes. Show him, Fargo."

Fargo dutifully grabbed Crimp by the hair and lifted him up so Digger could better see the bullet hole. Fargo looked up to the heavens and muttered under his breath, "Lord forgive me for this one."

"I done that?" Digger asked, sounding very impressed with himself.

"You did," Thornton said. "And you're gonna hang for it."

"You cain't hang me without a trial. I knows that much," Digger said.

"I forgot to tell you," Thornton said. "We held the trial while you were still knocked cold."

"How'd I do?" Digger asked eagerly.

"We brought you in guilty," Thornton said.

"Oh," Digger replied. Then he asked, "Where's Lila Mae?"

"We got her locked up in a root cellar on the other side of town," Thornton lied. "Figured it would be too tough on her seeing her brother dancing on the end of a rope."

"Yer bluffing," Digger said.

"Take a look outside," Thornton said. "You'll see if we're bluffing."

Digger managed to half stand on the cot and look out the barred window. Sure enough, Mushy was throwing a rope over a gnarly old oak tree in the town square. Digger's roan stood nearby, contentedly chewing some hay. Digger swallowed hard and felt his neck.

"You hang at sunset, about five hours." Thornton said. "Unless you tell us where Ma's at."

"I ain't tellin' you shit," Digger said.

Fargo bolted across the room and into the cell. He pulled his Colt and jammed it halfway down Digger's throat. Digger, his eyes wider than two fifty-cent pieces, tried to keep from gagging.

"You don't know me, but I'm Skye Fargo," Fargo said to him. "I've killed my share of sidewindin' scum like you, so one more is just so much velvet. I'll look you straight in the eye, pull this trigger and watch your head explode like a watermelon. So either you tell me where your ma is holed up, or you're dead.

"One," Fargo said, cocking the trigger. "Two—"

"Mummmph mumph," Digger gurgled excitedly. Fargo yanked the barrel of the gun out of Digger's mouth.

"Cottonwood Lake, south of the Snake River," Digger said breathlessly. "That's where Ma said they'd be."

He wasn't a bad liar, all things considered. Having the barrel of a Colt rammed down his gullet was likely not a first-time experience for the likes of Digger Purdy. Also, weasels like Digger never told the truth the first time around, no matter what the circumstances. Lying wasn't just second nature to the boy; it crossed the finish line first by ten lengths. Serious measures were needed.

Fargo fired a shot into the wall, right below the window and an inch from Digger Purdy's ear. The roar of the gunshot filled the room. The bullet passed close enough to take a small chunk of Digger's right earlobe with it. Digger cried out and slapped his free hand against the side of his head as blood spurted through his fingers.

"Now I'll take the truth," Fargo said.

Digger started blubbering, snot running from his nose and tears leaking from his lifeless eyes. "You shot mah ear off!" he cried out to Fargo.

"Stop being such a baby," Fargo said, and aimed the Colt a couple of inches from Digger's crotch. "Lie to me again and I'll shoot off something even closer to home."

"The South Loop territory," Digger said, trying to stem the flow of blood from his ear. There was a lot of it, though the wound was relatively minor. "Near Broken Bow. I swear it!"

"How many men in the gang?" Fargo asked.

Digger counted off the five fingers of his left hand, concentrating to the best of his limited ability, then switched to his right, which was sticky with blood. He counted off all ten, then instinctively tried to reach for his toes to continue to count.

"That's plenty," Fargo said, getting the general idea. A dozen, maybe more. "You best not be lying, boy. If you are, I'll come back and finish what I started."

"It's the truth, Mister, I swear," Digger said. "But you never know with Ma. She's kinda contrary sometimes. Says she'll be one place, ends up in another."

"How far is this South Loop territory?" Fargo asked Thornton.

"Half a day's ride," the marshal said. "Know how to get there?"

"No need to," Fargo said. "I'll follow Lila Mae. Ma will find her. Best get Mr. Belinsky over here to patch up this coyote."

Belinsky, suddenly appearing behind them, said, "Not necessary. When I heard the shot, I decided to be in the neighborhood."

"There's your patient, Jacob," Thornton said.

"He *shot* me!" Digger wailed, pointing to Fargo.

"Of course he shot you!" Belinsky responded, as he went into the cell and started mopping up the blood on Digger's face and hands. "You were expecting maybe a proposal of marriage?"

Fargo went to saddle up. Thornton said, "I hope you know what you're doing, Fargo."

"Get in line," Fargo said.

After Fargo rode off, Thornton told Mushy Callahan to go down to the stable and pick out a good horse for himself, and bring along Thornton's own mount, saying, "My gut tells me Fargo's riding into trouble. He may need help."

Lila Mae's trail was more than four hours old, but Fargo had little trouble tracking her. She had made no attempts to cover her trail, which meant that Lila Mae didn't care whether she was being followed. She'd crossed the creek a mile or two south of Flatwater, then headed due east. Freshly bent branches and broken twigs attested to her path. Fargo followed her trail into a more deeply wooded section of land.

Thornton had insisted on coming along, but Fargo preferred to go this one alone. The people of Flatwater were running scared, with many deciding to clear out altogether until the plundering Purdy gang was gone. Thornton would be needed more to quell the rising tide of hysteria. Seeing Thornton hold his ground would reassure them a little, anyway.

Fargo urged the Ovaro down a slope choked with

deadfall and deeper into the woods, which provided some relief from the heat. The sun was starting to set; Fargo estimated he was three, maybe four miles behind her.

An hour or two later, the sight of her horse, without her on it, brought him to a halt. He dismounted, drew his Colt, and made his way over to the roan. Something wasn't quite right with this picture—Lila Mae was nowhere to be seen. Despite this, he knew instinctively that he wasn't alone.

Above him was a towering oak tree. Fargo sensed a shadow falling on him, and looked up. Too late— Lila Mae, perched on a limb, dived off and landed squarely atop him. The Colt flew out of his hand as they crashed to the ground together. Lila Mae wrapped her fingers around his throat. Her hands were surprisingly strong. He grabbed her wrists and had to work hard to pry them off his windpipe. Lila Mae managed to free one hand and dug her nails deeply into Fargo's face. He popped her solidly on the chin, stunning her just long enough to roll on top of her.

She slithered like a rattlesnake beneath him, and he had his hands full keeping her pinned there. She tried to knee him in the groin; but he'd anticipated that move and managed to wiggle sideways to avoid her leg. She kicked her legs out from underneath him, trying to connect with any part of his body and inflict as much pain as possible.

She was a handful, this one, and as Fargo pressed his weight against her, damned if he didn't find himself getting highly aroused. Hard not to, considering her firm, plump breasts were rubbing against his chest. They rolled around the leaf- and twig-covered ground before Lila Mae, on top of him now, managed to get one arm free and produced a knife from inside her boot. He wondered dimly where she'd gotten it. She did her best to bury the blade in his side; Fargo grabbed her wrist and gave it a firm twist, then whipped her hand sideways. Lila Mae cried out in agony as the knife went flying deep into the forest.

Fargo rolled back on top of her, pinning her arms to the ground again.

She writhed and wiggled under him. Fargo, to his chagrin, could not control his stiffening steel. A man's rod sometimes had the annoying habit of coming to attention when he least wanted it to.

"You're as hard as a rock, big man," Lila Mae huffed. A few drops of blood splattered on her face, Fargo realized with some horror, from the gouges she'd carved in his cheek. He still had her pinned to the ground. At this point, she had pretty much stopped struggling.

"Take me now," she gasped. "Do me, you egg-sucking coward."

Lila Mae licked her lips invitingly. Fargo's erection showed no signs of easing up, which didn't make things any easier. To do as she wanted went against everything he believed in—she was an outlaw, a killer, but damn if she wasn't a lot of woman. Her nipples were threatening to burst through the thin fabric of her sweat-soaked shirt.

Lila Mae didn't help matters by wrapping her legs around him and rubbing her crotch against the big lump in his pants. Fargo started to sweat.

Fargo was still deciding the best way to handle this unusual turn of events, when the decision was made for him. So distracted was he by Lila Mae's sexual charms, he never heard or saw a thing until he felt the cold metal on the back of his neck.

"Leave her go, mister, or I'll blast you into the middle of next week," came the voice behind him.

Fargo sighed and cursed the day he'd set foot in Flatwater, Nebraska Territory.

Bill Dill pointed the rifle an inch from Fargo's forehead as Lila Mae wrapped the ropes around him, binding him across the chest to the tree. She tied him up nice and tight against the old elm tree, loving every second of the task. His Colt was tucked neatly inside the belt of her blue jeans; his Henry rifle was propped up against a tree. The Ovaro was grazing contentedly a few yards away. Fargo had never felt so helpless in all his born years.

"I did good, right?" Bill Dill asked Lila Mae.

Lila Mae said, "You did just fine, Billy."

"Did he have his way with you, Lila Mae?" Bill Dill asked her.

Lila Mae walked around the tree, lashing the rope around Fargo's neck. She then went to his Ovaro and tried to lead the animal closer to the tree where Fargo was lashed down. The pinto reared up on his hind legs, snorted wildly, and tried to kick Lila Mae in the head. She backed away, then moved in and smacked the horse squarely on the snoot with her left fist. The horse quickly became submissive. Lila Mae wrapped the other end of the rope around the horse's neck and tied a quick knot. If the Ovaro got restless or tried to bolt, Fargo was a dead man.

Fargo said, "Why don't you just kill me now, girl?"

"You shut up, peckerwood," Bill Dill said, slamming the butt of his rifle onto Fargo's head. Fargo fought off unconsciousness despite the fireworks that were going off in his head.

Lila Mae ignored them both, finishing the job with the rope. She went to Bill Dill's horse and rooted through the saddlebags, tossing out a can of peaches, some tobacco, a couple of bullets, and a rotten ham sandwich wrapped in a stinky handkerchief.

She turned to Bill Dill and said, "Where's the money, darling?"

6

Bill Dill dutifully put down his rifle and reached into his pants. He yanked out a bulging leather bag and said to her, "Got a nice chunk of it, Lila Mae. Almost four thousand in paper and gold coins. It was right on her, Lila Mae, just like you said it would be. I had to wait till she went off into the woods to drop a load. Cracked her over the noggin twice with the butt of my pistol. She's one hard-headed old buzzard, your mama is. We can make love now, right, Lila Mae? Like you promised?"

"Now ain't the time, you jar head," she snapped. "We best put some miles between us and Ma."

"That old bag of bones ain't goin' nowheres, girl," Bill Dill said. "I told you, I had to clunk her on the head with the butt of my gun, three times. Pretty sure I caved in her skull. There were lots of blood. She might be dead."

"Don't bet the farm on it, Billy," Lila Mae said dubiously. "You don't know Ma."

Bill Dill's eyes turned into dark, angry slits. "Yeah," he responded, grabbing her arm, and not gently. "And you don't know me."

He held her tightly against his chest and wrapped his massive arms around her. Lila Mae squirmed like a greased piglet in his powerful grasp.

"We made us a promise, girly girl," Bill Dill said. "I kept up my end, now you're a-gonna keep up yours."

"I will, Billy," Lila Mae said, attempting to free herself and getting nowhere. "But there's my brothers, too—"

Bill Dill said, "I ain't afraid of your idiot brothers, nor anyone else. Let 'em come. I'll blast their worthless hides into the middle of next week. You're a-gonna give it up, and give it up now. Get them clothes off or I'll rip 'em off my ownself."

He released her. Lila Mae looked over at Fargo, her eyes pleading for help, not that he was in a position to do much. He shrugged, as if to say *you got yourself into this mess, girl. You're on your own.*

Lila Mae pulled off her dirty shirt, her breasts flopping out in all their pert glory. Bill Dill's eyes lit up like twin bonfires. Even Fargo, who'd seen his share of well-endowed ladies, couldn't help but be impressed.

Bill Dill started drooling, eyeing her with a savage hunger. He said, "Lay down, girl," and started unbuttoning his blue jeans. They fell to his ankles. Lila Mae chose that moment to turn and run. Bill Dill growled indignantly and tried to run after her, getting no more than a few steps before he tripped over his own britches and fell facedown into the dirt. Lila Mae scrambled over to where Fargo was bound up and frantically tried to untie his ropes.

Bill Dill was up and on her in seconds, grabbing a fistful of her hair. He dragged her kicking and screaming into a clump of bushes and fell on top of her. "A little cock teaser, that's what you are," Bill Dill said, as Lila Mae struggled under him, punching his back and arms. "But you ain't a-gonna cock tease me no more." He hauled off and slapped her hard, and her struggling stopped.

"You got a real smooth way with the ladies, Billy," Fargo commented from the sidelines. "Next time try some roses and a bottle of fizzy wine."

"Shut up, you," Bill Dill said, and went about the business of yanking her tight pants off. Lila Mae lay there lifelessly, or so it appeared—until she sprang up and sank her choppers into Dill's left ear. Even from twenty yards away, Fargo saw the blood spurt. Bill Dill howled in pain and backhanded Lila Mae a second time.

"Bitch!" he snapped, and rolled her roughly onto her belly, then wiped the blood from the side of his head. "Just for that, I'm a-gonna give it to you where the sun don't shine." He'd already made the decision to kill her and the strange man tied to the tree after he'd taken his pleasure. He'd travel faster alone.

Fargo strained at the ropes, but Lila Mae and her new boyfriend had done a first-rate job of tying him up. He could do nothing but sit and watch this animal have his way with her.

Before Bill Dill could violate her, though, the man screamed in pain. At first, Fargo wasn't sure why until he saw Dill pull something out of his leg—a bowie knife, it looked like. Blood spurted from the wound. Dill yelped in pain and sat down hard and made a dive for his holster. A shot rang out and the holster skidded across the dirt. Bill Dill belly crawled toward it, but it was too late. Another shot rang out and found a home in Bill Dill's left shoulder. He cried out in agony and rolled onto his back.

Fargo saw a small Indian appear from out of the woods—Cherokee Sam, he dimly recalled from an old wanted poster. He was followed by a bunch of the meanest plug uglies he'd seen on a hundred different wanted posters from Tennessee to West Texas. All of them were toting the latest fashions from Smith & Wesson. Ma Purdy chose her men well, he'd give her that much. There were seven or eight of them that Fargo could see, and that was enough to last a lifetime.

Then he saw her. Mother Purdy. The old hatchet face was very much alive. Her wanted poster actually did the old girl a degree of justice. She was even uglier up close.

Ma Purdy didn't look happy. The party was over. Pistol drawn, Ma strode over to Bill Dill, who was frozen in terror, his eyes bulging hideously.

"This ain't—ain't—what it looks like," Bill Dill stammered.

"I'll tell you what it looks like," Ma said and shot him squarely in the left knee, which exploded into a small red cloud of meat and bone chips. Bill Dill howled in agony and rolled onto his side, clutching his wounded leg. Blood poured through his fingers.

She said to him, "There's gonna be hell to pay, son, and you're pickin' up the tab."

She took off her hat to fan herself. A bloody rag was pressed over the wound in her head, caused by Dill's gun.

Ma Purdy walked over to Lila Mae and prodded her with the tip of her boot and said, "Get your britches on, you ignorant slut. You want the boys to see y'all nekkid?"

Brother Sherman picked up her torn shirt and threw it at her, a look of disgust on his face. Sister or no sister, Lila Mae was bad news, always kept his teeth on edge. He didn't see where she was doing them much good.

Lila Mae quickly put her shirt on and pulled up her pants, saying, "He tried to rape me, Mama. Stole all your money, too. He told me so—it's right in my saddlebag, I wuz gonna bring it back to y'all, Ma—"

Ma slapped her hard. "Don't be makin' it any worse by lyin', girl," Ma said, and ordered Coffin Ike to fetch the money. "You tricked that sorry son of a bitch into stealin' my money and promised to light out with him," Ma Purdy said.

"Mama—" Lila Mae started.

"Shut up," Ma said, and moved on to more weighty issues, asking her, "Did he poke you, girl? Did he put it all the way in? Are you soiled goods?"

Lila Mae started weeping, though not all that convincingly, "He tried, Ma, but—"

Ma whacked her across the face again, leaving furious red welts on her cheek. She bellowed, "I ast you a question, girl! Did you give it up to him?"

"No!" Lila Mae screamed back, then spit into the dirt.

"Well, fine," Ma snapped, and added, "You think you can hornswoggle your old ma? Old Billy here ain't got the smarts to think this one up. Ain't that right, Billy?"

Bill Dill, clutching his wounded leg, moaned, "That's right, Ma."

"You wuz gonna run off with my only daughter and my hard-earned money," Ma said. "Whooped me on the head pretty good, too. I'm powerful mad at you, Billy."

"Lemme kill him now, Ma," Sherman Purdy said eagerly, cocking his pistol.

Asa Miner, Strap McClure, Jonah Hardsock, and the others looked down at Bill Dill with a combination of disgust and pity—disgust, because he'd been dumb enough to think he could get over on Mother Purdy. Pity, because when Ma got done with him, there wouldn't be enough left over to feed a horsefly.

Ma ignored Sherman and asked Lila Mae, "Where's Digger?"

"Over to Flatwater," Lila Mae said. "They're fixin' to hang him, if they ain't already."

This bit of news did not put Ma Purdy in a better humor. She said to Lila Mae, "And you left him there to get hung? So's you could run off with this piece of dirt?" She pulled a Colt from under her belt and shot Bill Dill in the right kneecap. Gristle and blood decorated his face and chest. His screams filled the dusk, music to Ma's ears. She bellowed at her daughter, getting good and mad now and capable of inflicting the tortures of the damned. "If anything's happened to your brother, Lila Mae, so help me Jesus—"

"Your boy is still alive," Fargo piped up.

"Who's him?" Ma asked Lila Mae.

"I'm the man who stands between your son and the noose around his scrawny neck," Fargo said.

"Don't listen to him, Ma," Lila Mae said. "He—"

"Shuddup," Ma barked at her. She said to Fargo, "Who are you, stranger?"

"Skye Fargo, and if I ain't back in Flatwater by sunup, without any bullet holes in me and still breathin', Digger's gonna dance on air."

"How do I know he ain't already dead?" Ma wanted to know.

"You don't," Fargo said. "Reckon you'll just have to trust me."

"You ain't in no position to be givin' orders, stranger," Ma said. She walked over and put the barrel of the pistol squarely on the tip of Fargo's nose.

"Kill me and you'll never see your precious Digger again," Fargo said.

"And what if I don't care?" Ma asked, cocking the pistol.

"If you didn't care," Fargo said, sweating despite the faint chill in the air. "I'd be dead already."

"You're as good as dead now, stranger," Ma said, then asked Lila, "The town know we're headed their way?"

"They do now," Lila Mae said. "Digger made sure of that, gettin' drunk and shootin' up half the town."

"Killed a man, too," Fargo added, and immediately wished he hadn't. Ma turned to him again and gave him a look that could wither a field of daisies. She turned back to Lila Mae and said, "Where they holdin' him?"

"Where else would they hold him?" Lila Mae answered. "In the goddam jail!"

"Now," Ma said to Fargo, "you gonna call my daughter a liar?"

"Not if I can help it," he said.

"Then she's tellin' the truth?"

"She was," Fargo said, "but the marshal moved him, and I don't know where."

"Then you ain't much use to me, are ye now?" she said, aiming squarely at his chest.

Fargo was about to offer up and answer to that when he saw Mushy Callahan, hidden in a brush-choked washout a hundred yards away, aiming a Winchester rifle right at Ma's broad back. The next split second would decide Fargo's fate.

7

Mushy fired, but his shot went a little wild, hitting the dirt a few feet from where Ma stood. Yet it did the trick. Ma dived for cover, as did all of her intrepid band of merrymakers, seeking refuge behind trees.

"Ambush!" someone cried, and two dozen shots from the guns of both Mushy and Deke Thornton ripped through the dusk. The Ovaro reared up in fright, tightening the rope around Fargo's neck. Breathing was no longer an option. Fargo wriggled and squirmed and finally managed to get one hand free. He got a finger or two under the rope, which was slicing into his windpipe. A little more excitement and the Ovaro would separate him from his head.

Meanwhile, Ma and her boys fired blindly into the woods, into the direction Mushy's shot had come from—unaware, of course, that Mushy and Thornton had fanned out in opposite directions. They fired once, twice, and then moved on, making it seem, in the confusion of the moment at least, that there were six of them instead of two. It was just dark enough now for Thornton and Mushy to pull it off.

Fargo struggled furiously with the ropes as his Ovaro strained at the other end. Fargo slid his entire hand under the rope. The Ovaro reared up again, the smell of gunsmoke driving the animal insane with fear.

The rope tightened even more, pressing Fargo's hand hard against his face, blocking his mouth and nose. *What a stupid way to die,* Fargo thought, fighting to stay conscious.

Bullets flew in from everywhere. Asa Miner, not very well concealed behind a tree stump, took a hunk of Thornton's lead in the left side of his head. The bullet tore downward through his brain, what little there was of it, and exited through his chin, taking most of his jaw with it. Miner flopped over sideways and was dead before he hit the dirt.

Fargo continued struggling with the rope, but it appeared to be a losing battle. Lila Mae belly crawled over, toting his Henry. She whipped out a knife and started slicing through the rope furiously. Fargo didn't know why she'd chosen to help him, but was grateful.

In the midst of the firefight, with the Purdy gang shooting wildly into the night, brother Lumbert the idiot, unconcerned or unaware that bullets were whizzing by him, ambled into the middle of the clearing, clutching a dead frog in his fist.

Ma cried out, "Hold yer fire! Don't shoot Lumbert!"

All shooting ceased. Lumbert plopped himself down and started playing with the dead frog, drooling like an infant, saying, "Froggy! Good froggy."

"Lumbert," Ma barked in a show of motherly love, "get your crazy ass out of here!"

Lumbert ignored her and tried to put the frog up one nostril. When this failed, he stuffed the frog into his mouth and started squealing delightedly.

"Get that frog out of your mouth this minute, boy!" Ma cried at him.

Thornton, behind a live oak, was close enough to

see the idiot kid munching the frog, two little green legs poking out of his mouth. "What the hell," Thornton said to himself. The kid was directly in the line of fire; Thornton couldn't bring himself to blast an idiot kid, even if he *was* a Purdy.

Slicing the rope as fast as she could, Lila Mae said to Fargo, "My brother eats frogs, and you wonder why I wanna get as far away from them as possible?"

Lumbert got up and shuffled off to parts unknown. Ma cried out, "Okay, go ahead!" The firefight started anew.

Lila Mae finally managed to cut through the cords. Fargo sucked in air, filling his grateful lungs.

"Thanks," Fargo croaked. He had an angry red gash around his gullet that would smart like hell in the days to come, but it beat being dead.

"Don't thank me yet," Lila Mae said. "I didn't save your miserable life 'cause I'm a nice person."

"Oh?" Fargo asked, and swallowed hard. "And here I thought it was my irresistible charm."

"Not likely," Lila Mae said. "You're a-gonna take me with you, big man." She handed him the Henry.

Fargo grabbed it, and his Colt from her belt, too. He said, "Then let's go if we're goin'." He grabbed her hand and they scurried off into the brush. Fargo whistled, and the Ovaro trotted dutifully off behind them. There was enough gunplay that their escape went unnoticed—almost. Ma saw them slipping away and hollered, "You git back here, you evil little slut!"

She aimed and fired at Fargo, missing him by an entire two inches. More bullets followed, and Fargo found himself pushing at Lila Mae, prodding her to keep moving at a steady clip. She tripped over a tree root and tumbled to the ground. Fargo, in turn, tripped over Lila Mae and went flying. He tumbled a few times and landed against the base of an elm tree. When he focused his eyes, Mushy Callahan was standing over him, ready to shoot first and ask stupid questions later.

Fargo said to him, "Hold your water, you old buzzard."

"That you, Fargo?" Mushy asked, aiming straight at Fargo's head—some things never changed.

Pushing the barrel of Mushy's rifle away, Fargo said, "Now who the hell else would it be?"

Mushy raised his rifle again, this time at Lila Mae, and would have blasted her into eternity had Fargo not pushed the rifle barrel away again. "Shit on fire and save the matches, Fargo," Mushy said, with some heat. "She's a Purdy—let me kill her."

"Not today," Fargo told him, getting to his feet and cocking the Henry. "For the time being, she's with us."

Mushy wasn't convinced. He said, "And after you've had your way with her, then what?"

"Well, we won't get into that now," Fargo said. "What the hell are you doing here?"

"I could ask you the same question, old son," Mushy said, spitting tobacco juice into a shrub. He aimed and fired into the woods, hoping to hit anything Purdy.

"Is Thornton with you?"

"You think I'd come out here alone?" Mushy asked, as he fired off another volley. He started to move again. Fargo grabbed Lila Mae's arm and took off after Mushy, liking the idea that the old buzzard had figured smart enough to employ the hit and run routine.

The Purdy gang started retreating back into the woods to regroup. Ma cried out, "Someone grab Lumbert, goddamn it!" She saw Bill Dill writhing around on the ground, everything below the waist looking like a freshly slaughtered pig. She trotted over and said, "Ain't got the time to kill you the way I'd really like to. More's the pity."

"No . . . Mother Purdy . . . please," Bill Dill begged.

"Oh sweet limpin' Jesus, die like a man," Ma said, and pumped two shots into his head—one in each eye.

Deke Thornton watched Asa Miner die and remembered something his father, gone these last twenty years now, said to him once, when Deke was a boy of twelve.

"It don't really matter what you do in this life, son," the old man had said as he pushed that rickety plow through the barren, rocky Tennessee topsoil. "Just be the best Deke Thornton that you can be. That's all anyone, includin' the Almighty, has a right to ask."

Deke Thornton had just killed one of the vicious Purdy gang, and to his way of thinking, that made him the best Deke Thornton he could be. He'd been a lawman for most of his adult life, had helped clean up some of the most notorious hellholes from Kentucky to Wyoming Territory; had faced down some of the meanest, badest desperados to ever draw breath. He'd kept the peace in charming little burgs with names like Black Ear, Missouri; Cut Lip, Arkansas; Dead Dog, Kentucky; and Gadzooks, Kansas—all small towns with big, bad reputations. He'd leaped at the opportunity to work in Flatwater, Nebraska Territory; a small, peaceful little town, where a runaway mule on Main Street had thus far posed the most danger.

Ma and her boys were scattering now. Time to move on. He hadn't seen Mushy, but the old coot had a talent for survival. He squeezed off one last shot at someone running through the dark woods and missed.

He turned to run and felt the knife slam into his belly before he could even see the small Indian wielding it. Thornton's rifle fell to the ground. Cherokee Sam gave the blade a hefty twist, churning up Thornton's insides, then yanked it out. He vanished into the trees as silently as he'd appeared.

"Son of a bitch," Thornton croaked. He clutched his belly, blood squirting through his fingers, and fell to his knees. He toppled over sideways, feeling the life drain out of him. He was still in that position when Fargo, Mushy, and Lila Mae came upon him.

Fargo rolled Thornton onto his back and asked, "Where'd they get you?"

"In the belly," Thornton said weakly. Blood was pumping out of the hole in his gut. "Little redskin bastard bushwhacked me."

"Cherokee Sam," Mushy said.

Fargo grabbed Thornton's arms, meaning to sling him over his shoulder and carry him back to his Ovaro. Thornton said, "Leave me be, Fargo. I've had it."

"Nobody dies on me," Fargo said, but the truth was all too evident.

As Mushy tried to soak up the blood from the marshal's wound, Thornton asked, "Why is it, Skye Fargo, that my life went straight into the shitter the day you rode into Flatwater? Stole my girl, made me look like a fool, brought the damn Purdys down on me."

"Wasn't anything personal," Fargo said.

"Bullshit," Thornton said, and coughed up blood. "It doesn't get any more personal than this."

Thornton coughed again, and died, his eyes still open. Fargo closed them and whispered, "You done good, Thornton."

Furious now—a good lawman was dead—Fargo grabbed Lila Mae's wrists and said to her, "I'm telling you now, little lady: I ain't gonna rest until I blast your ma and all the Purdys straight into hell."

"Then you're a-gonna need a damn good plan, big man," she said. " 'Cause y'all got Ma's blood up, and there ain't no stopping her now."

"I've got a good plan," Fargo said to her, "and you're part of it."

8

In their absence, Digger Purdy had escaped from jail.

Thornton had left Jacob Belinsky in charge when he and Mushy went after Fargo. Around six that evening, about the same time Fargo was being choked near to death by his own horse, Digger mentioned to Jacob, "Ah'm gittin' hongry."

Belinsky said, "Yes, I would think killing people works up an appetite."

A little food, Belinsky reasoned, couldn't hurt anything. He went to the café and returned with fried chicken, biscuits, beans, apple pie, and a glass of buttermilk.

"Such greasy food they have in the West," Belinsky commented as he set the tray down in the cell and loosened the ropes around Digger's wrists. "Everything fried—not a goodness." Since arriving in Flatwater two years earlier, he'd waged a one-man campaign to get Emma and Lars to cook up some cheese blintzes and matzoh ball soup, to no avail. Placing the plates down, Belinsky said to Digger, "You should do me a favor and not eat the tray. Lars needs it back."

Digger reacted through the bar, taking the glass and heartily gulping down buttermilk. Tearing into the meal, Digger said, "You know, ah never kilt no one."

"Oh? I heard different," Belinsky said. "I heard you and your mother and our brothers have killed a lot of people. You're what they call a *desperator,* am I correct?"

"I think y'all mean desperado. Sure, we kilt some, I reckon," Digger replied, popping a biscuit into his mouth. "And when Ma and the rest get here, we're goona blow your butt off, too."

Belinsky was sitting at Thornton's desk. Digger sat on the floor, eating like an animal, shoveling the vittles into his mouth as fast as he could. Bean juice dribbled down his chin.

"Such nasty language you use," Belinsky said, then asked, "So when did you kill your first person?"

"Ain't none of yer goddamn business," Digger said with a snarl.

"I'm not asking for business," Belinsky said.

"Was thirteen, I think, on my birthday," Digger said. "Ma made me do it. A feller behind a teller's cage, in Texas." He tore into a chicken leg. "After we got the money, Ma said to me, 'Digger, it's time you lost your cherry.' She put the gun in my hand and told me to shoot the man."

"And you did?" Belinsky asked in astonishment.

"Sure," Digger said. "Weren't much. Hit him right in the throat. Ma was proud as a peacock. That night, she gave me a whole bottle of whiskey to drink for my ownself."

Belinsky clucked his tongue and said, "When a Jewish boy turns thirteen, he gets a bar mitzvah. When a Purdy turns thirteen, he gets a gun. Oy, this is some country!"

Digger devoured the chicken, bones and all. He

belched audibly and said, "I could shore use a smoke."

"A smoke he wants," Belinsky snorted. "Maybe I could shine your shoes, too?"

Digger ignored the question, asking, "They really fixin' to string me up?"

Belinsky shrugged and said, "They don't tell me anything, and I don't ask. A very nice arrangement. Hanging, oy! Me, I don't believe in it, but if hanging makes you crazy Westerners happy, then go with God. You wouldn't by any chance be scared, would you, Mr. Desperado?"

"I ain't scairt of shit," Digger said, sounding a little more defiant, thanks to a full belly.

"Not even a little?"

"You ask a lot of questions, mister," Digger said.

"So you're late for a church social, maybe?" Belinsky asked.

"You talk funny, too, like you're from someplace else."

"Isn't everyone in America from someplace else?" Belinsky asked now.

"Y'all want the tray back?" Digger asked. "I'm finished."

"Thank you," Belinsky said. "Just one more question, Mr. Desperado: It doesn't bother you that I just took too bullets out of a very nice man who never harmed anyone?"

"No," Digger said, picking his teeth. "Why should it?"

"Why should it, he wants to know," Belinsky muttered. "America, such a *meshuggameh* land. Kindly slide the glass you used under the cell door, please."

"Don't think it's a-gonna fit," Digger said, surveying

the space between the floor and the bars on the cell. "See? You best come on in here and get it."

"You want I should come in there with you, all untied?" Belinsky asked. "Listen to me, my very new friend: Jacob Belinsky is not a coward, but neither is Jacob Belinsky a schmuck. You'll kindly hand the glass to me through the bars. Can we try that?"

Digger stood and handed the glass to Belinsky. When his hand was empty, Digger lashed out like lightning and grabbed a handful of Belinshy's beard and yanked his face into the metal bars with a sickening thud. Belinsky saw bright, beautiful stars, momentarily stunned. Digger smashed Belinsky's face into the bars a second time, then snaked his arm through the bars and curled it around Belinsky's neck. The glass fell from his hands and shattered all over the floor.

"You a-gonna let me out, or do I strangle you right here?" Digger asked, holding Belinsky in a death grip.

Blood cascading out of his nose, the world spinning, Belinsky managed to say, "Let you out . . . ?"

"Gimmee the key, or I'll snap your neck," Digger said. "Makes no matter to me I kill one more afore they hang me." He tightened his grip on Belinsky to drive home the point.

The cell-door key ring was hanging on a hook about four feet away. Belinsky reached for it and fell short by three or four inches.

"Too far," Belinsky said hoarsely.

"You just ain't tryin' hard enough, is all," Digger said, and with his other hand grabbed Belinsky's hair and clunked his head against the bars.

Belinsky felt dizzy for a minute, but it passed. He said, "We'll never get anywhere if you keep doing that."

112

He reached again, stretching his skinny arms as far as nature would allow. His fingertips brushed against the key ring, but they still weren't close enough to grasp.

"You'll have to loosen your grip," Belinsky croaked.

"I do that and you'll slip away," Digger said. "I ain't no schmork, neither."

"That's open to discussion," Belinsky said, knowing full well this crazy little *pisher* would kill him and think nothing of it, as if swatting an annoying bug. He reached out again, hearing things pop in his arm as he stretched it with everything he had inside. But he still couldn't quite make it. Digger grabbed Belinsky's outstretched arm and stretched it a little more. Pain shot through Belinsky's shoulder. The tips of his fingers touched metal keys.

"Grab 'em," Digger ordered, almost pulling Belinsky's arm clear out of the socket.

His face turning the color of pickled beets, Belinsky grunted and somehow lifted the key ring off the hook, where it sat precariously on the tip of his forefinger.

"Real slow now, bring it over here," Digger instructed.

As directed, Belinsky brought his hand back. When it was a few feet from the cell, Digger reached out to grab the keys. They slid off Belinsky's finger and clattered to the floor three feet away.

"Lookit what y'all did," Digger said angrily.

"What *I* did?" Belinsky asked indignantly. "You couldn't wait two seconds, no, not you."

"Now what in the name of Jesus are we supposed to do?" Digger asked angrily.

"What Jesus would do, I couldn't say," Belinsky replied. "As for me, I'm open to suggestions."

"Get down," Digger said, pressing his hand on top of Belinsky's head, and together they sank to the floor, his arm still wrapped around Belinsky's neck. "Now reach out with your foot and get them keys back here."

Belinsky kicked out and managed to drag the keys back to a place where Digger could grab them with his free hand.

"Okay, up," he said, and together they rose to their feet, Digger clutching the keys. When they were standing erect, Digger jammed one of the three skeleton keys into the lock. When that one didn't work, he tried another When that one didn't work, either, Digger snapped. "Damn! Goddamn!"

"Patience is a virtue, Mr. Purdy," Belinsky said.

He tried the third key, and heard something click. Digger pushed the cell door open, shoving Belinsky halfway across the room where he crashed violently into the desk.

"Such a *putz* I am!" he lamented. Digger paid him no mind, tossing the keys aside and making a beeline toward the gun rack, which in someone's haste—Mushy's, most likely—had been left unlocked. Not that there was much worth taking; an old Hawken rifle and a somewhat rusty six-shooter. Digger took them anyway, tucking the pistol into his belt. He rummaged through Thornton's desk, found a box of cartridges, and stuffed them in his pocket.

Belinsky said, "Better you should stay here. They're not going to hang you, not really. And just how far do you think you'll get without a horse?"

"I wuz plannin' on stealing one," Digger said, adding, "You seem like a nice enough feller, Jacob. It's a gol-darned shame I gotta do this."

He slammed the butt of the Hawken against Belinsky's head, knocking him cold. He dragged Belinsky inside the cell and slammed the door. Except for the huge knot on his forehead, Belinsky looked almost peaceful, all laid out on the floor.

Looking down at him, Digger said, "Takes all kinds of folks to make a world, mister. Especially suckers."

"This don't look too promising, do it?" Mushy Callahan said to Fargo when they got back to the jail. Belinsky was sitting on the bunk, rubbing the bump on his forehead and looking downright sheepish.

Fargo opened his mouth to speak. Belinsky held his hand and said, "If you were planning on making me feel bad, don't bother. There's nothing you could say that would make me feel any worse!"

"When?" Fargo asked.

"An hour, maybe more," Belinsky said. "Who can remember, with all the yelling and the hitting and the unpleasantness."

Fargo, Mushy, and Lila Mae looked down at the shattered glass and plates, which pretty much told the whole story. Lila Mae asked Belinsky, "Don't tell me y'all *trusted* that little shit bird?"

"Ain't your fault, Mr. Belinsky," Fargo said, hunting for the keys and finding them beside the potbellied stove. "You just trust people too much." He unlocked the cell and added, "You're over it now, I suspect."

"I tol' Thornton not to leave a tinhorn in charge," Mushy said. "Just askin' for trouble, Deke was, Lord rest his soul."

"Deke's resting his soul?" Belinsky asked, wide-eyed. "You mean—"

" 'Fraid so," Fargo said. "Ain't none of us too happy about it."

"Poor Mr. Thornton," Belinsky said, sinking heavily into a chair. "I can't believe it. Such a good man. Was it the Purdys?"

"Yeah," Fargo said bitterly. "The ever-lovin' Purdys."

"You best get your ducks in a row, tall man," Lila Mae piped up. "This town's done stuck its nose in biggest hornet's nest this side of the Mississippi."

Fargo turned to Mushy and Belinsky and said, "You best gather up as many of the townsfolk as you can. Bring them all over to the church."

"Good idee," Mushy said.

"And Mr. Belinsky," Fargo added. "Would you be so kind as to fetch Miss Lundegard over here."

Belinsky nodded, then asked, "What have we done to deserve this?"

"Just lucky, I guess," Fargo said.

"In the old country there were the Cossacks. Here in America, they call them Purdys," Belinsky said. "Oy, what a world."

9

When Sara saw Jacob Belinsky and the grim expression on his bearded face she suspected the worst. He stood on the porch, hat in hands, a black skullcap plastered to his head.

He said, "You better come with me now, Sarah."

"Oh, my God," Sarah said. "Jacob, is it—?"

"I'm afraid so, dear," Jacob said, his eyes misting up. "A brave man. He gave his life for this town."

Sarah's shoulders slumped; her face crumpled in grief and tears dribbled from her eyes. She wept into a lace hanky. Belinsky awkwardly put his arms around her. Sarah sobbed and sniffled and shuddered against him.

"A tragedy," Belinsky said as Sarah continued sobbing. "Poor Deke. He—"

Sarah pushed herself away from Belinsky, no longer weeping. "Deke? I thought you said Fargo was dead!"

"No," Belinsky said innocently. "Mr. Fargo is fine. Just a nasty rope burn around the neck."

Sarah sat down hard on the top porch step. She'd never felt so mixed up in the head in her life. Lars and Emma came to the door. "Jacob—what happened?" Lars asked.

The Purdy people killed Mr. Thornton," Belinsky said.

Emma gasped.

"Mr. Fargo wants to see us all over at the church, for an emergency meeting," Belinsky said.

Sarah was crying again. Her aunt Emma sat down beside her and tried to comfort her, obviously unaware—unlike everyone else in Flatwater—of Sarah's passionate tryst with Fargo. Lars, too, it seemed was ignorant on the subject, for he commented to Belinsky, "Sarah was in luff with Deke Thornton, by jiminy."

"Yes," Belinsky said dryly. "I'll see if I have any black dresses from Mr. Sears and Mr. Roebuck."

Sarah gave him a look but said nothing.

"What on God's green earth is *she* doing here?" Sarah asked when she saw Lila Mae, who was washing her face in a bucket of water. Mushy Callahan had managed to find a bottle of whiskey and was doing his best to suck down every last drop.

Even with wet hair and covered in several layers of grime, Lila Mae looked good. Lord help me, Fargo thought, there was something about the girl that made his manhood get hard just looking at her.

"Lila Mae has decided to renounce her life of crime and walk the straight and narrow path of righteousness," Fargo said.

"Mule fritters!" Sarah snapped. "She's one of them, for corn's sake. Have you lost your mind, Skye?"

"You can't lose something you never had," Fargo said, and damn if Sarah wasn't just a little bit jealous. "Lila Mae's on our side now. The Lord works in mysterious ways, Sarah."

"In a pig's poke," Sarah said. "She's evil white trash, the lowest kind of prairie vermin."

Lila Mae lifted her head out of the bucket and asked Fargo, "Who's she?"

"Miss Lila Mae Purdy," Fargo said, "please meet Miss Sarah Lundegard."

"I don't think I like her," Lila Mae said.

"Why, you vicious little slut, don't you dare speak to me in that tone," Sarah said, charging at her. Lila Mae was greased lightning, grabbing the bucket and splashing gray water all over the floor. She went at Sarah with the single-minded intention of smashing the bucket over her head. Fargo snatched the bucket from Lila Mae and pushed her away. At the same time, he caught Sarah around the waist. She squirmed in his arms, wanting nothing more than to bury her fingernails in Lila Mae's face.

Lila Mae charged again, her eyes ablaze with shrewd, merciless, animal cunning. She grabbed Sarah's long blonde hair and yanked hard. Sarah wailed in pain and jammed some fingers into Lila Mae's eyes. Fargo did all he could to keep them apart, but it was a losing battle. Sarah had all but wriggled out of his grasp and nothing less than her blinding Lila Mae would do.

"Feel free to jump in and help me anytime," Fargo said to Mushy.

"And stand in the way of true love?" Mushy asked, and took a big swig from the bottle. Cain't recollect the last time I had two women fightin' over me."

Fargo managed to pry them apart momentarily. Lila Mae kicked Fargo in the left shin, hard. He buckled to his knees and fell to the floor. Sarah and Lila Mae had at it, trying to choke each other. Lila Mae punched Sarah smack on her nose and at the same time kicked her in the knee, just as she had kicked

Fargo. Sarah collapsed on Fargo's belly, knocking the wind out of his lungs. Lila Mae dived onto Sarah's back and grabbed a clump of hair, almost ripping it from Sarah's skull. Fargo struggled to push the battling women off his stomach, getting nowhere. Mushy wisely chose that moment to come to Fargo's aid. He tried to grab Lila Mae by her chin and the top of her head to pry her off of Sarah. Lila Mae sank her razor-like choppers into two of Mushy's fingers, biting down to the bone. Mushy cried out in pain and fell over backward, clutching his wounded hand.

Fargo squirmed out from under them. Lila Mae and Sarah rolled all over the floor, locked in mortal combat, their catfight now going in earnest.

"Just couldn't wait to get your filthy hands on him, could you?" Sarah screamed at Lila Mae, who responded, "Kiss my foot, you blonde bitch. You fucked him first and don't say otherwise. It's wrote all over your face."

Sarah spit in Lila Mae's eye. The kicking and biting and gouging continued. Under different circumstances, Fargo might very well have enjoyed the spectacle of two pretty young ladies rolling around on the floor. But not here and now. He drew his Colt and fired two shots into the ceiling.

The fight ended abruptly. Out of breath, Fargo said, "Fight's over, dammit! Save your strength, for Chrissakes."

Lila Mae and Sarah looked at each other, sisters in arms for one brief moment. Then Lila Mae grabbed Sarah's head and gave it one good slam against the floor, just for the hell of it.

"Goddamn it, Lila Mae, stop that!" Fargo demanded. "Sarah, take Lila Mae over to the café. Boil some water and make some bandages. We'll be needing them soon enough. And make coffee. Lots of it."

"Fine," Sarah said, stomping off. "But from here on in, Mr. Skye Fargo, don't climb up that oak tree outside my window, because I won't be waiting for you. Not ever." She turned to Lila Mae and said, "Well, come on if you're coming." She disappeared out the door.

Lila Mae asked Fargo, "When do I see you again?"

"Go help Sarah," Fargo said. "We'll discuss it later."

"You can bet on it, mister."

Before she left, Fargo asked her, "Lila Mae—I got one question for you, and I'd be eternally grateful if you answer it as honest as possible."

"And what would that be?"

"Knowing your ma as you do, when she runs roughshod over a defenseless town like this one," he asked, "when does she usually choose to do it?"

"Tall man," Lila Mae said, "the only predictable thing about Ma Purdy is, she's always unpredictable."

She gave Fargo's crotch a healthy squeeze. It was painful and pleasant both. "See you later, lover," she said.

Nursing his bloody hand, Mushy Callahan said, "You do have a way of keeping the pot simmering, Skye Fargo."

"Make life interesting, don't it?" Fargo responded. "We best get over to the church now."

"This ain't your fight, Fargo," Mushy said. "You ain't got to stay."

"The hell I don't," Fargo said. He thought of Sarah Lundegard naked in the moonlight. It was a pleasant image. He said to Mushy, "Guess I got my foot caught in the door again."

"I guess you did," Mushy said.

Lumbert Purdy loved spitting into the fire and watching it sizzle on the hot coals. The little red embers were so pretty. Lumbert wanted to play with one. He started to reach into the fire to grab one when Coffin Ike grabbed his brother's hand and clunked him on the skull.

"Fire ain't for playin' with, you turnip head," Ike snapped.

"Let the boy be," Mother Purdy. "He don't know what he's doin'."

It was a few hours after sundown. They'd buried Asa Miner, but left Bill Dill and Deke Thornton for the buzzards. Digger had found his way to the camp earlier, and for that Ma was happy. What made her very unhappy was Lila Mae's running off with that Skye Fargo. Lila Mae was valuable goods, and Ma wanted her back.

They were sitting around the campfire now, passing around some bottles of whiskey. As per Ma's rules, only members of the immediate family were allowed to discuss business. There was always some grumbling from the nonblood members of the gang, but not too much. Even if her sons were all dumber than a sack of beer suds, a seasoned outlaw always made good money riding with Mother Purdy, and usually had some fun, too. The trick was not to get killed—that really was the key to reaping the benefits. It was the main reason Ma never seemed to have much trouble recruiting new talent after one run-in or another with the law. After supper, Jonah Hardsock, Strap Mc-

Clure, Micah Gorr, and Cherokee Sam drifted off into the night while Ma made plans.

Sherman asked, "Are we a-gonna hit this town or not, Ma? It ain't like we got all the time in the world."

"A little before dawn," Ma replied. " 'Bout seven hours, give or take."

"Why don't we just charge in there now and blast 'em all?" Ike wanted to know.

"That's right," Digger said, liking the idea. "I got me a score to settle with those people. You know what they done? They—"

"Shut yer stupid mouth," Ma said, taking a hefty pull from the bottle and wiping her chins on her sleeve. "You damn near spoilt everything, gittin' drunk an' shootin' up the town. You and yer dumb sister led 'em right to us."

"That's right," Ike said. "Damn near got us all kilt. From now on, you do as Ma says, else I'll whip the tar outta ya!"

"You go to hell, you shit heel!" Digger shouted at his brother. He hated it when Ike tried to boss him around.

"Kiss mah rosy-red ass cheeks, you ignorant peckerwood!" Ike stormed back.

Digger dived at his brother across the fire, knocking Lumbert off the log. Lumbert fell backward and hit his head on a rock. He started bawling and had himself a little spastic fit. He was ignored as Digger and Ike fought in the dirt, punching and biting each other. Ike got Digger in a headlock and punched his face repeatedly, the blows bouncing off his nose until blood started coming out of it. Digger grabbed Ike's left ear and tried to rip it clear from his head. Ike bellowed in agony and punched at Digger's hand, in effect punching himself in the head. The fight would have lasted indefinitely, had Sherman Purdy not grabbed the kettle of bubbling beans off the cook fire and slopped the contents all over his brothers. Digger and Ike both howled in pain as the sizzling hot beans rained down on them.

"Like Ma told y'all," Sherman said, taking charge now that Ma was too drunk to care. "We go in an hour before dawn. The more time those pig farmers, the ones dumb enough to stay around, have to think about what we're gonna do to them, the more scared they're gonna get. That's the time to hit 'em—when they all tired and frightened. And that's when we're goin' in. Not a moment sooner. You two sissy boys got any objections to that?"

They didn't.

Reverend Eustace Q. Tilley, of the Little Flower Methodist Church of Flatwater, Nebraska Territory, tried in vain to keep the proceedings orderly. Half of Flatwater's two hundred or so residents had arrived; others were arriving in drips and drabs as Mushy Callahan, like a grizzled, whiskery Paul Revere, galloped from farm to farm alerting folks of the Purdys' impending arrival.

Old biddies in pink bonnets cackled on the edge of hysteria. The men passed bottles back and forth—Reverend Tilley tried to ignore this blasphemous activity—heatedly discussing the situation as little children ran excitedly up and down the aisles. Purdy fever was sweeping Flatwater like a plague of locusts. Deke Thornton's death had thrown the townsfolk into a tizzy; it had unnerved virtually everyone in town.

Luther Heggs, a one-legged rancher from the north

end of the territory, said to Dud Kissel, "Kill 'em all and let the Almighty sort 'em out, that's what I say!"

There were cheers and shouts of agreement.

"May we please have some order!" Reverend Tilley boomed in his loudest Sunday sermon voice.

"Me and the missus, we're clearing out till this blows over," said a farmer named Aaron Fleagle. His wife, Agnes, nodded vigorously in agreement, adding, "We think it would be for the best. I've heard that these Purdy people are not decent Christians."

There were echos of agreement from the other townspeople. Benjamin Cheerstrap, who owned the bakery and prided himself on his creampuffs, piped up, "Fleagle is right. How can we ever hope to defend ourselves against the Purdy gang? I'm packing up my family and heading for Ogallala or maybe Scottsbluff. Maybe when this is all over—"

"You gutless pukes!" Luther Heggs cried, clutching a bottle of whiskey. He was half drunk, as were his two sons, Alvin, age twenty, and Lester, twenty-one. "Ain't no Purdy gang gonna run me off my ranch, that's for goddamn certain!"

"Mr. Heggs," Reverend Tilley said severely. "Please remember you're in the house of the Lord."

Sitting in the back of the church, Fargo said, "Leave if you're of a mind to, but there won't be any coming back, not for anybody. The Purdys'll burn Flatwater to the ground and laugh about it later. Is that what you good people want? To see everything you've worked a lifetime for destroyed in the space of a few hours?"

"Maybe they'll just rob the bank and leave," Norval Stoon offered hopefully. Henry Twerk, the banker, glared at him.

"Not a chance," Fargo said. "With the Purdys, past experience has shown us to hope for the best but prepare for the worst. Make no mistake—the Purdys are a small army, and only one thing can stop a small army: a bigger army."

"An army? Most of the men in this town have never even fired a gun, for goodness sake," Henry Twerk said. "What chance would we have against the Purdys?"

"That's right," Dud Kissel agreed. "I say we pack up and hightail it out of here."

"Then you might as well keep running," Fargo said.

There were more murmurs of agreement. Shelby Oathammer, a farmer from the northern part of town, said, "We don't see you coming up with any ideas, Mr. Fargo."

"That's right," Norval Stoon chimed in. "Who elected you the new marshal, Fargo? Who are you to tell us what to do?"

"You're absolutely right," Fargo replied, feeling a little hot under the collar. "Nobody elected me anything, and I have no right to ask you to risk your lives. But let's keep the record straight on one little item: You people seem to forget that this ain't even my fight. I was just unlucky enough to find myself in this little slice of heaven when the Purdys decided to pay you a visit. So just say the word and I'll be on my way."

Henry Twerk nervously wiped his bald pate with a hanky. He, better than anyone, knew how high the stakes were. In addition to the bank, he owned pieces of half a dozen businesses in town. "Now don't lets be impetuous, Mr. Fargo," he said.

Twerk then pointed to Aaron Fleagle and said,

"How much are you into my bank for your farm, Aaron?" He pointed to Shelby Oathammer and asked, "And you, Shelby—who gave you more time on your note after them grasshoppers devoured all your crops last July? I'm holding paper on damn near every spread in this territory. I could've called in those notes anytime I saw fit and tossed you all off your land. But did I?"

"No," Shelby Oathammer said, "but that didn't stop you from jacking up the payments, did it, Henry Twerk?"

The other farmers agreed. Henry Twerk liked a dollar and made one any way he could. Jonah Wilbershot, another local, said, "You're askin' us to die for a few lousy acres that don't produce much even in the best of times. No, sir," he added. "Me and my family, we've been happy here, I don't deny that, but it just ain't worth dyin' for."

"That's just peachy," Twerk said. "Go on, get the hell out. But you all remember this: I didn't invite the Purdy gang to Flatwater. So when you let those murdering bastards run you off your spreads, when you can't get a bolt of cloth or a sack of flour for the missus or penny candy for your younguns because they burn Jacob Belinsky's mercantile to the ground; when there's nowhere to buy a drink or get a haircut and a shave, or even a place to worship under the hands of the Good Lord; when it all turns to deep, dark hell, don't shed your tears on my doorstep and expect me to take you back with open arms. You leave, and you forfeit everything."

A swell of yelling and cursing erupted in the small church. Things were getting out of hand. Reverend Tilley tried to calm the good people of Flatwater, to no avail. Finally, Fargo drew his Colt and fired a shot into the ceiling, a move that never failed to get the people's attention. A hush fell over the congregation.

"We live in a harsh land, folks, an untamed frontier," Fargo said. "And what's happening here today could happen anywhere. There's a time to run, and there's a time to fight. You lay down for the Purdys today, you'll be opening the door for any prairie scum in the West who thinks he can come in here and pillage and poison what's left of your town. You were right when you said I got no stake in what happens here—I don't, not really. But I do have a stake in the future of this land. And what happens in Flatwater in the next few hours will play a big part in the lives of your children and great-grandchildren.

"That said," Fargo went on, "I got me a plan that just might get us through this. If we band together, we can outnumber 'em by three to one. There ain't enough cover out of town to mount an ambush, so it looks like we'll have to take them right here on Main Street. I'm tellin' you now: Some of you might get hurt; some of you might even get yourselves killed. But if we pull this off right, I think we got a pretty good chance."

"What y'all got in mind, Fargo?" Mushy Callahan asked.

Fargo looked at Luther Heggs and asked, "How many head of cattle you got, Mr. Heggs?"

"Over a hundred," he said. "Why? You plannin' a barbeque?"

"Not exactly," Fargo said. "How soon can you move 'em into town?"

"What the hell fer?" Heggs asked, but then it slowly dawned on him what Fargo had in mind, and he said, "By sunup, I reckon, if we get a move on."

"Then I suggest you get a move on," Fargo said and asked Mushy Callahan, "Where's Mr. Belinsky?"

"Over at his store, I reckon," Mushy said.

"Okay," Fargo said, swinging into action. He asked Mayor Twerk, "I want you to get the children and womenfolk off someplace safe, as far out of town as possible. The Purdys'll be riding in from the east; is there anywhere west of town they can hole up till this is over?"

"Sure," Twerk said. "We can send them over to Ash Hollow—it's perfect. A small valley, surrounded by big oaks. They ought to be safe there."

"Then you best get 'em going," Fargo said. To the men of Flatwater, Nebraska Territory, he said, "I want you all to go home and get whatever firearms you got, doesn't matter what, and be back here in an hour, no later."

Reverend Tilley asked, "What can I do, Mr. Fargo? I'd like to help out any way I possibly can."

"Thank you, Reverend," Fargo said. "Have you prepared your sermon for this Sunday yet?"

"Why, yes," Reverend Tilley said. "In fact, I finished it earlier this week."

"Good," Fargo said. "You're gonna get a chance to use it. Just sit tight and wait till I come back."

Fargo turned to Mushy and said, "Let's pay us a visit to Mr. Belinsky."

"What you all got up your sleeve, Fargo?" Mushy asked. "I'd feel a mite better if I knew your plan."

"So would I," Fargo said. "I'm making this up as I go along."

"Was a-feared of that," Mushy said, and followed him out.

10

"Lard?" Belinsky asked. "You want lard? What for? You're planning on baking a cake maybe?"

"No," Fargo said patiently. It was after two in the morning; precious minutes were slipping away. "I want you to take it over to the café and boil it up— and keep it boiling."

Fargo went into the back room, which doubled as both Belinsky's living quarters and a supply room. Samuel Pruett Drinkwater was dozing peacefully on Belinsky's goose down mattress.

"Give me a hand with him," Fargo said, and together he and Mushy lifted Drinkwater off the mattress. The snake-oil salesman barely stirred.

"You *shmendricks,* what are you doing?" Belinsky cried out. "He's not a well man."

"We need your mattress, Mr. Belinsky," Fargo said.

"Lard he wants, my beautiful goose down mattress he wants," Belinsky said. "So much I don't understand."

"And I don't have time to explain it now," Fargo said, "Where can we put him?"

"I don't know," Belinsky said, pacing frantically around the room, looking for something to rest Mr. Drinkwater on. Fargo and Mushy followed him, lugging the motionless salesman.

"C'mon, Jacob," Mushy said. "This man ain't gettin' any lighter."

They set Drinkwater down on the floor inside the bed frame. He snorted once and continued dozing. Fargo said to Mushy, "Give me your knife."

Mushy handed Fargo his blade. Fargo ripped the mattress down the middle—feathers spurted all over the storeroom in a small blizzard.

"Oy *gevalt*!" Belinsky cried. "That mattress came all the way from Chicaggi!"

"Sorry, Mr. Belinsky," Fargo said. "But it's for a good cause."

"Cause *shmause*," Belinsky said.

Fargo grabbed a bunch of burlap sacks and handed them to Belinsky. He said, "Fill these with feathers, Mr. Belinsky, and take them over to the café if you'd be so kind."

"The more I know," Belinsky muttered, gathering up the feathers and stuffing them into the sacks as instructed, "the less I understand."

"Okay," Fargo said to Mushy. "Let's head on back to the church and see what the good men of Flatwater are made of."

As they were leaving, they heard Belinsky say sarcastically, "Chopped liver."

By four a.m., Flatwater was as ready as it would ever be. It was a cloudy night, maybe two hours before dawn. Fargo knew in his gut that the Purdys would strike within the next two hours, at the latest. Mushy Callahan had ridden out, heading east per instructions, and was to ride hell to leather back at the first sign of the Purdys. The women and children had been shepherded out of town to the place called Ash Hollow and, hopefully, safety. Norval Stoon and his sons had rounded up as many head of cattle as they could and were herding them, with some difficulty, right outside the west end of Flatwater.

Fargo's instructions to the menfolk were simple and straightforward: "Shoot at anything that moves." The men scattered to their assigned posts all over Main Street. He went over to the café where, as directed, Sarah and Lila Mae were making bandages and Jacob Belinsky was boiling up the lard. Emma and Lars were frying steaks and scrambling eggs, although few in town felt like eating.

"You all best leave now," Fargo told the women. "Things are likely to start percolating any time."

"Then you'll need us here," Sarah said. Lila Mae agreed, as did Lars and Emma.

"Ya, when da Purdys come, us you will need," Emma echoed.

Fargo would have none of it, saying, "Too dangerous. You've done all you could. When them bullets start flying, anything's bound to happen, and it probably will."

"But Skye—" Sarah started to say.

"It ain't a request, Sarah," Fargo said.

Fargo left before any of them could protest further. Toting his Henry and his Colt, he made his way over to the Flatwater Hotel across from the church. He opted for a second-floor room that gave him a wide view of the street.

He settled down under the window and tried to fight off the weariness that was creeping over him. It occurred to him that it had been two days since he'd last slept, and Lord, did that nice bed look inviting. Most of the men in town were probably feeling the same way; it was something the Purdys would very well try to exploit.

Fargo waited and tried not to fall asleep. The town was dead silent—even the crickets seemed to sense the impending bloodbath and had wisely moved on to a less busy location. Five minutes passed, and the next thing Fargo remembered was Lila Mae shaking him awake. Fargo snapped to full consciousness. Grabbing the Henry, he asked, "Are they here?"

"Not yet," Lila Mae said, handing him a steaming cup of coffee. "Thought you might need this."

Fargo gratefully accepted it and asked her, "What the hell are you doing here? I thought I told you to leave."

Lila Mae sat on edge of the bed. She said, "I was studying on what you said before—about how maybe we might all die. Got me to thinking."

"Did it now?" Fargo asked.

Yes," Lila Mae responded. "I don't wanna die a virgin."

Fargo's eyes widened. "A virgin? You?"

She nodded shyly. Fargo said, "I wasn't born yesterday, honey. If you're a virgin, then I'm Christ on the cross."

"Ma worked hard to keep me pure," Lila Mae said. "Had plans for me, she did."

"All right, so you're a virgin," Fargo said, in no mood to argue with her. "What do you want me to do about it?"

Lila Mae giggled and pushed off her suspenders.

"Oh, no," Fargo said. "It ain't the place, and it sure as hell ain't the time."

"We ain't a-gonna get anywheres with y'all sittin' over there and me sittin' over here," Lila Mae said.

She pulled her shirt off, exposing a pair of mouth-watering melons that made Fargo start drooling in spite of himself. The moonlight bathed her in an amber glow; sex rolled off her in waves. She had nipples like two plump, juicy red cherries standing firm.

Fargo stood and said, "This just ain't—"

Lila Mae reached out and grabbed his arm, yanking him with surprising force, flinging him down onto the bed. She leaped on top of him, straddling him, those bodacious breasts swinging perilously close to his face.

"You know what to do, big man," Lila Mae said, and kissed him passionately on the mouth. She slid her hand under his shirt and ran it up and down his chest.

"Lila—" Fargo tried to say, but she kissed him harder to shut him up. Her hand creeped down to his crotch, slipped under his pants, and began to fondle his throbbing member. The kiss ended. Fargo felt something warm, wet, and wonderful on his shaft and could see Lila Mae's head bobbing up and down.

"Where did you learn how to pleasure a man like this if you're a virgin?" Fargo asked breathlessly.

"Seen Ma do it once or twice," Lila Mae said, and went back about her business. Fargo barely managed to keep that particularly nasty image from flitting across his mind, concentrating instead on Lila Mae's most talented tongue.

He was one lick away from surrendering completely to her. He'd regret it forever if he didn't feel those luscious breasts against his chest at least once again in his lifetime. He grabbed Lila Mae around the waist and flung her down onto her back. She squirmed out of her britches and lay naked under him. Fargo kicked his jeans down around his ankles and rolled on top of her. Lila Mae wrapped her arms around him and spread her legs wide.

"Take me now, big man," she moaned. "Do me."

Fargo brought himself to her, burying his shaft in her moist womanhood. Lila Mae moaned deeply, running the soles of her little feet down the lengths of his legs. She kissed him again, jamming her tongue halfway down his throat as he thrust his hips, sliding into her even more deeply.

"Oh, it feels soooo good," Lila Mae gasped, writhing in ecstasy under him. True to form, she buried her sharp nails into his back and dragged them across his hard, tightly muscled flesh. Fargo gave one last thrust and exploded. Lila moaned breathlessly under him. They climaxed simultaneously, arms and legs entwined.

"Virgin my butt," Fargo muttered under his breath.

They were catching their breath when there was a single knock on the door. It opened, and in came Sarah Lundegard, holding a tray of food and a coffee cup. Behind her, clutching an impossibly bright lantern was her aunt Emma.

"Skye? We just thought you'd like something to—" Sarah started, then got a jaw-dropping gander at the scene on the bed: Fargo, with his pants down around his ankles, was lying atop Lila Mae Purdy. Sarah's mouth hung open, trying to form a syllable or two. The tray slipped from her grasp, sending chicken sandwiches and coffee splattering all over the floor.

Finding her voice, Sarah said softly, "Skye, how could you?"

"He didn't need a hell of a lotta persuadin', honey," Lila Mae said, and chuckled.

Sarah turned and bolted out of the hotel room, taking the steps to the lobby three at a time. Fargo called out after her, "Sarah—would you believe me if I said she doesn't mean a thing to me?"

"What the hell's that supposed to mean?" Lila Mae asked angrily. Her fist shot out and connected with Fargo's nose.

"Ow," he squawked, feeling his nostrils for blood. Lila Mae pushed him away and started gathering up her britches and her shirt. Fargo grabbed the bedspread and threw it across his bare crotch.

Aunt Emma asked, sounding slightly disgusted, "Why always do men think with their *schmeckles*?"

Fargo had no answer for that.

11

The Purdys rode in with the very first rays of the morning sun.

A few minutes earlier, Mushy Callahan had galloped back into town. Fargo met him at the jail. Mushy said excitedly, "Done looks like they've arrived. Counted nine of 'em, includin' the idiot frog eater."

"Okay," Fargo said. "You know what to do."

Mushy nodded and made his way inside the church and climbed up into the steeple. There was barely enough room between him and the massive bell Reverend Tilley clanged every Sunday morning.

Nine abreast, Mother Purdy and her gang of cutthroats approached the outskirts of Flatwater. They sat tall and erect in their saddles—all except Lumbert, who was strapped belly down onto his, his head lolling against his horse's side.

Ma Purdy held her arm out silently, motioning for the boys to halt. The gang surveyed the deserted main street of town, which at this early hour was eerily silent. There were no signs of life anywhere, not even a chirping sparrow.

Wide alert and guided by a razor-sharp cunning, Ma immediately sensed something amiss. These corn-fed jaspers knew Ma and her boys were coming. Had they cleared out, leaving them to pillage the town at their leisure?

Ma didn't quite think so. She scanned the tops of the buildings for flashes of gunmetal or a person's hiding head and saw nothing.

Suddenly, five hundred yards away, a deep baritone voice came booming out of the church, sermonizing from the sound of it—something about Jesus and lying down with a lion and a lamb. The voice echoed throughout the deserted town. Ma motioned for Micah Gorr to take a look.

Gorr dismounted and made his way over to the church. He drew his pistol and kicked open the church door. On the pulpit, Reverend Tilley was waving the Good Book and preaching to a congregation of nobody. The damn place was deserted.

"Just what the hell you think you're doin'?" Micah Gorr asked.

"Come to Jesus, join the flock, dear brother!" Reverend Tilley boomed. "Hear the word of the Lord and receive everlasting forgiveness!"

"Not much hope of that," Micah Gorr said, almost amused at the spectacle of this crazy man preaching the gospel to a couple of church mice. "Not much of a turnout today, eh, preacher?"

"Oh, you'd be surprised," Reverend Tilley said.

Jonah Wilbershot and Shelby Oathammer popped up from behind the front row of pews, pistols drawn, and fired two shots apiece at Micah Gorr. Three of them went wild, slamming into the wall on either side of him. The fourth shot hit Gorr in the left shoulder. Gorr was knocked backward but still managed to squeeze off two shots of his own, one of which caught Shelby Oathammer squarely in belly.

Oathammer dropped to the floor, clutching his stomach. Wilbershot squeezed off another shot, missing Gorr by a good eighteen inches. Gorr fired back, winging Wilbershot's right forearm. Reverend Tilley dived off the pulpit for Oathammer's gun. In his enthusiasm, he smashed headfirst into the front pew but somehow managed to get his hands on the hunk of hot steel. He cocked the pistol and fired and cried, "Help me now, Jesus!"

Whether through divine intervention or just plain luck, the bullet hit Micah Gorr in the chest, the force of the shot spinning him around. He staggered out the church door and onto Main Street.

"Lord forgive me," Reverend Tilley said.

"Screw that!" Wilbershot cried. "Finish what you started, Reverend."

Ma cried out, "It's a bushwhack, boys!" Spurs hit flanks and the Purdy gang scattered all over Main Street, galloping every which way. Micah Gorr, looking for all the world like a Saturday night drunk, staggered around in middle of the street but refused to go down. From the steeple, Mushy aimed his carbine and fired. The bullet kicked up some dust around Gorr's feet.

"Damn," Mushy said. "Ain't the shot I used to be." He slapped another bullet into the chamber, fired, and missed again. He was about to reload when he saw Reverend Tilley fly out of the church, raise the pistol, and fire at Micah Gorr. He caught the outlaw in the throat. Gorr gave up the ghost and sank to his knees, fell forward and lay still.

"Forgive me, Lord, for shedding the blood of my fellow man," Reverend Tilley said.

From atop the steeple, Mushy Callahan yelled at

him, "Ain't no need to apologize, you dumb Jesus-jumpin' bastard!"

Shots rang out from the rooftops. The good men of Flatwater, with one or two exceptions, missed their targets on the street below. Fargo, from the second floor of the hotel, cursed silently. Mother Purdy had gambled that the townsfolk were incapable of hitting the broad side of a barn, and her gamble was paying off. Fargo managed to wing Jonah Hardsock in the shoulder, knocking him off his horse. Hardsock scurried away and disappeared down the alley between the bakery and the café. Otherwise, the Purdys were drawing most of the blood. Atop the livery stable, Fargo saw Aaron Fleagle clutch his belly and pitch forward off the roof. Digger Purdy rode up and pumped a few more shots into Fleagle's lifeless body. Fargo took aim at Digger—the little bastard was on a stolen horse, if things weren't bad enough—and was about to fire when Lila Mae, in a panic, threw her arms around his neck and cried out, "Don't let them get me, big man! Ma will kill me fer sure!"

Fargo tried to pry her arms from around his neck before she strangled him.

"She won't kill you if I can kill her first, you damn fool," Fargo snapped. He took aim again out the window, fired, and struck, Lumbert's horse in the hindquarters. The horse flopped over, sending Lumbert flying into the street. Lumbert sat up and started blubbering, tears streaming down his dirt-caked face.

Over at the church, Mushy was ringing the church bell frantically. At the west end of town, Luther Heggs and his sons, Alvin and Lester, heard the clanging of the bell, their cue to swing into action. Luther whooped and hollered, and together, the three of them fired their guns into the air, spooking the hundred head of cattle. The herd panicked and started stampeding straight down Main Street, directly into the path of the marauding Purdys. Luther Heggs and his sons rode in behind the herd.

"Stampede!" Ma Purdy cried as the frightened cattle thundered down the street and even the wooden walkways, kicking up a huge cloud of brown dust that blotted out the sunlight almost completely, adding to the overall pandemonium. She spurred her horse around, having lost sight of her sons, and rode hard toward the opposite end of town. She heard Sherman cry out behind her, "Ma—Lumbert!"

Ma Purdy jerked the horse to a halt and looked back. The cattle were cascading down the street directly at Lumbert, who sat serenely on his ass, sucking his thumb, completely oblivious to his impending doom. Bullets raining down on them from everywhere, Ma and Sherman watched in horror as six thousand pounds of terrified prime beef trampled Lumbert flatter than a griddle cake. Ma fired into the oncoming herd, more out of rage and frustration than anything else, and dropped a couple of the steers.

From atop the steeple, Mushy took aim at Sherman and said to himself, "Gonna have us one hell of a barbeque when this is all over." He squeezed off a shot and scored a direct hit—into one of Luther Heggs's prize heifers.

Fargo watched all of this from the hotel room. He said to Lila Mae, "Get down in the cellar and lock the door behind you. Don't come out until I tell you. Whatever you hear, whatever you see, don't come out until I come back for you, understand?"

Lila Mae nodded and flew the down the stairs to

the cellar. He went back to his post at the third floor window and started shooting, without success, at Coffin Ike and Strap McClure, who were darting between buildings.

Jonah Hardsock, meanwhile, dismounted at the end of the alleyway adjacent to the café and kicked the kitchen door open with his boot. Lars was huddled under a long wooden table, atop of which sat a huge washbin used for cleaning dishes. Hardsock drew his six-guns, wanting nothing more than to kill someone—anyone. Lars looked at the six-guns pointed at his head and shut his eyes, waiting to die and wishing he'd never left the old country ten years earlier.

From behind Hardsock, Sarah came out swinging a fifteen-pound cast-iron frying pan and connected with the back of Hardsock's thick skull, which made a sickening splattery sound. His head spinning, brains scrambled, Hardsock whirled around and saw two Sarahs instead of one. He fired at the Sarah on the left, but instead of hitting her, the bullet went wild and ricocheted off a copper pot hanging from a rack next to the enormous griddle. From there, the bullet pinged off a second copper pot and careened crazily back in the same direction it had been fired. Jonah Hardsock felt something slam into his forehead, an inch above his left eye. Hardsock continued standing momentarily, stunned, then staggered sideways toward the oven, where a huge pot of water was still boiling. He grabbed the burning hot pot handle as he fell to the floor, pulling the pot of boiling water off the stove. A second after he hit, the pot tipped over, spilling the boiling water all over his face and chest and cooking his flesh instantly. He let out a howl of pain, thrashing wildly as blood spurted out of the hole in his head.

The whole watery red mess sloshed all over the floor as Hardsock writhed in agony. He did a little death rattle and died with his eyes still open, his flesh-seared face frozen in a mask of agony.

"Is he dead?" Lars asked his niece.

Sarah picked one of Hardsock's pistols off the floor, cocked it, and fired twice into the lifeless body. Hardsock's corpse jerked a couple of times then stopped.

"He is now, that's for damned sure," she replied.

As Luther Heggs was stampeding his cattle down Main Street, trampling Lumbert Purdy to death, Jacob Belinsky was running from behind the café to his mercantile, toting two large buckets of boiling lard. Waiting on the roof already were a couple of sacks filled with the feathers of his precious goose down mattress. He was to take them to the roof of his store and drop the stuff onto the nearest Purdy gang member, which would have sounded crazy from anyone but Skye Fargo, Jacob Belinsky had come to trust him as much as he could trust any man.

Jacob set the pails down and opened the back door to his mercantile. He picked up the pails and dashed into the storeroom/living quarters. He got no farther than six inches inside when a leg shot out beside him and tripped him. Jacob fell flat on his face, the buckets flying out ahead of him, spilling the hot lard. The back door slammed shut. Belinsky rolled onto his back and saw Digger Purdy standing over him, pointing the barrel of the Hawken inches from his nose.

"Howdy," Digger said. "Had a feelin' we'd be meetin' up agin."

"Hello yourself," Belinsky said, disgusted that Digger had gotten the better of him twice in one day. "Are you going to kill me?"

"What do you think?" Digger asked.

"For this I left Russia," Belinsky said. "You and your mother and your crazy brothers—you're nothing but a bunch of filthy Cossacks!"

"When I shoot y'all," Digger started to ask, "how do y'all want it? In the front or in the back?"

"Does it really make a difference?" Belinsky wanted to know.

"Not to me it don't," Digger said.

Belinsky tried to stall for time, asking, "Do you mind if I say my prayers first?"

"Ain't got time," Digger replied.

"You would maybe deny a dying man one last request?" Belinsky asked. "What kind of person does that?"

Digger rolled his eyes in exasperation and said, "Okay, go ahead. But make it quick. I got to kill y'all and get to the bank. Got money to steal."

"So young, yet so organized," Belinsky said, getting on his knees in a praying position, sort of swaying to and fro in a rocking motion. He started chanting in a language Digger had never heard. It wasn't Indian, and it wasn't Mexican. After a minute of it, Digger got bored and considered plugging the man there and then, prayers or no prayers. He didn't see Belinsky's right hand drop down to his shoe as he continued chanting.

"Okay, that's enough of that—" Digger started to say, and barely had time to react when Belinsky's right hand came up, a glint of metal clenched in his fist. Digger felt a white-hot bolt of pain shoot up his leg, saw the handle of the knife jutting out of his calf.

"You sidewindin' son of a bitch," he said, and felt himself falling, the Hawken slipping from his grasp.

He crashed to the floor, and then the bearded man was on him.

"I told you I wasn't a *schmuck,*" Belinsky said, and yanked the knife out of Digger's calf. He raised his arm up with the one goal of burying it in Digger's chest. Digger grabbed Belinsky's arm with one hand and clocked Belinsky on the chin with his other as hard as he could.

Belinsky toppled over sideways. The knife flew out of his hand and skidded across the floor. Digger lunged on top of him and started choking him, burying his fingers in Belinsky's throat.

"Stab a Purdy will ya?" Digger said, hatred seething through every syllable. Trying to pry those bony fingers from around his neck was useless, Belinsky knew after a futile attempt. His fingers groped around the floor for anything resembling a weapon, and finally closed around the handle of the tin pail after a few furtive attempts. He brought the heavy pail around and slammed it into the side of Digger's head.

Digger's grip loosened enough for Belinsky to push him away and scramble across the floor for the awkward Hawken, which he grabbed and aimed. Digger sat up and drew his revolver. They fired simultaneously, the dual explosions deafening. Problem was, the Hawken refused to function, Belinsky realized with great alarm as he heard the click.

Belinsky took a slug in the meaty part of his left arm. When the smoke cleared, he saw Digger still in a sitting position, looking down at a gaping, bloody hole in his chest. The revolver dropped from his hand. A shot had taken Digger dead center in the heart.

"You kilt me," Digger said weakly, "I thought you wuz my friend."

Breathing heavily and bleeding like a stuck pig, Belinsky replied, "I didn't shoot you. This *meshugganeh* gun doesn't work."

"The pleasure was all mine, dear sir," Samuel Pruett Drinkwater said from behind a stack of crates of canned peaches. He was holding a small Remington. "It was the least I could do for all your hospitality, Mr. Belinsky.

Digger keeled over into a dead heap, blood oozing from the hole in his chest.

Belinsky didn't know where Drinkwater had gotten the weapon, but at that point didn't much care.

"Oy, this America—what a crazy country," he said, and fainted dead away.

In the midst of all the shooting, Ma Purdy and her eldest son Sherman had taken temporary refuge in the church. Mushy's repeated shots at them had missed by a country mile. He tried to open the hatch door to the ladder that led down to the pulpit and found it jammed. He fired a couple of shots into it but still could not raise the latch.

"Son of a bitch!" he cried out in frustration.

Inside the church, Ma and Sherman found Reverend Tilley seeing to Jonah Wilbershot's wound. Shelby Oathammer was, retrettably, beyond any helping.

Ma put her gun to Reverend Tilley's head and asked, "Where's mah Lila Mae?"

"Who?" Reverend Tilley asked.

"Lila Mae!" Ma croaked. "Where in tarnation is she?"

Reverend Tilley looked utterly helpless until Wilbershot said, "She's talkin' about that slut daughter of hers. Don't tell her, Reverend!"

Ma shot Jonah Wilbershot point blank in the face, taking off a sizable portion of his head.

"Sweet Jesus," Reverend Tilley gasped.

"I'll only ask once again. Where is she?" Ma seethed.

"I think . . . the hotel . . ." Reverend Tilley said, a heavy blanket of shock engulfing him like a shroud. Seeing a goodly number of his loyal flock blown six ways from Sunday all over town was finally too much for him.

"Should I kill him, Ma?" Sherman asked.

"Cain't kill a man of God," Ma said to Sherman reproachfully. "Ah'll do it."

She put the barrel of her pistol up to Reverend Tilley's temple and pulled back the hammer. Tilley chose that moment to faint.

"Smart move, preacher," Ma said.

Coffin Ike Purdy and Strap McClure took cover behind a pile of grain sacks as Luther Heggs and his sons stampeded the last of the herd through town. They'd picked off two locals from the roof of the saloon, Norval Stoon among them. Nearly a dozen of his prize-blooded stock lay dead in the street. Luther Heggs was not a happy man. He rode pretty well for a one-legged man, though, better than his awkward sons. They galloped through town, trading lead with Ike and Strap McClure. Ike blasted Alvin Heggs out of his saddle with a single shot to the head, while Lester's horse, spooked by all the gunfire, reared up and sent him flying ass over teakettle onto the street, where he rolled every which way to keep from being trampled. Luther's mount went loco, bucking wildly, and Luther did all he could to hang on for dear life.

Ike and McClure went into the bank blasting away. The place was deserted. Someone had been kind enough to leave the safe unlocked, however. While Ike watched the door, Strap McClure yanked open the door to the safe. By the time he saw Henry Twerk, on bended knee and clutching a double-barreled shotgun, it was too late. Twerk let loose with a deafening volley that slammed McClure back against the teller's cage and killed him instantly.

"Rest in hell!" Twerk cried out gleefully.

Ike decided he didn't like the odds and made himself scarce. He ran like hell out of the bank and smack into one of Luther Hegg's snot-snorting prize bulls, which gored him in the belly, raising him a foot off the ground, and flipped him over. The bull—whom Luther Heggs had named Daisy in a drunken moment of whimsy—stomped on his head for good measure, spraying brains and blood all over Flatwater.

Then, suddenly, Flatwater was quiet again. The dust was settling. A few cows milled in the middle of Main Street amongst the dead bodies. Ma and Sherman ran out of the church and across the street toward the hotel. Mushy Callahan, still atop the steeple, saw them moving and called out, "Headin' your way, Fargo!"

Sherman turned around and fired at Mushy, hitting him in the torso. Mushy fell backward against the church bell, which started chiming. Fargo fired his Colt at them as they zigzagged across the street, making them difficult targets, until they disappeared from view.

Fargo scrambled out of the hotel room and down the stairs to the second floor landing just as Ma and Sherman blasted their way into the small lobby. Fargo raised the Henry and took a shot at Ma, who deftly dropped to the floor and rolled out of Fargo's gun sights. Sherman dived over the registration desk and came up firing. A shot thudded into the wall an inch from Fargo's nose, spraying wood and plaster in his eyes.

Fargo ducked a few feet down the hall, out of their line of fire, and reloaded his Colt. He snapped the cylinder shut and spun it for good measure. He crept back to the edge of the staircase, Colt raised. Two steps from the top of the landing, Sherman Purdy smashed the butt of his pistol against the bridge of Fargo's nose, knocking him to his knees. Damn, but that devil was quick, Fargo thought briefly.

Down, but not out, Fargo flung himself at Sherman's knees and grabbed them, throwing Sherman off balance. Together they tumbled down the stairs and crashed to the bottom in a heap, still grappling. They fell through the open door and into the street, locked in mortal combat.

On a hunch, Ma blasted the lock on the cellar door and shoved it open. She made her way down the stairs, her eyes adjusting to the darkness. Lila Mae sat cowering in a corner next to a bushel of dried corn.

"Mama, is that you?" Lila Mae asked. "Y'all come for me?"

"Don't give me any of that shit, gal," Ma said. "You ran off with that man, I knowed you did."

"Tweren't like that at all, Ma, I swear," Lila Mae pleaded. "He made me—"

"Made you is right," Ma snorted. "You been with him, ain't you?"

"No, Mama, he didn't," Lila Mae said. "He didn't do any such thing.

"You never could lie to me, Lila Mae," Ma said.

149

"You done and let him have at you. And I had such beautiful plans for you."

"No, Mama, I swear!" Lila Mae cried.

Ma raised her pistol and said, "I could abide you runnin' off, long as you were still pure when I got you back, but you ain't even that. You're worthless to me now, girl."

Ma aimed.

Fargo and Sherman Purdy were rolling around in Dud Kissel's carefully tended garden. Fargo pushed Sherman off, rolled sideways, and grabbed a wooden stake that had heretofore been supporting a withering tomato vine. Sherman leaped at Fargo, who lashed out with the stake just as Sherman landed on top of him. He felt the thin but razor-sharp wooden stake penetrate Sherman's throat, severing his windpipe and coming out the other side, shiny with thick blood. Sherman tumbled off Fargo and gasped desperately for air. He tried to pull the stake out with his ebbing strength. Fargo watched, as if in a trance, until the sorry spectacle of Sherman Purdy dying was interrupted by gunfire.

Fargo ran into the hotel lobby and saw the cellar door swinging open. He retrieved his Colt and waited, hiding behind the door. Two seconds later, Ma appeared at the top of the stairs and holstered her pistol. Fargo jammed the barrel of his Colt into Ma Purdy's spine.

"Drop the belt, Mother, real slow, and raise 'em up high," Fargo instructed.

Ma, knowing Fargo had the drop on her, unhitched her gun belt and let it fall to the floor. Fargo kicked her hard in the butt and sent her sprawling across the lobby. Ma fell at the foot of the stairs.

"Where's Lila Mae?" Fargo asked.

"Drop dead," Ma replied. "Was she good, Fargo? Did y'all enjoy deflowerin' my pride and joy?"

"I've had better," Fargo said and watched as Ma's black, soulless eyes filled with bitter hatred.

"What are y'all waitin' for, Fargo?" Ma asked. "Kill me and let's be done with it. I just don't give a rat's ass anymore."

"Oh, no," Fargo said. "You ain't getting off that easy. A lot of good folks are dead 'cause of you. No, you're gonna hang, and I aim to put the rope around your neck my ownself."

"You little scum-sucking prick," Ma said. "Nobody hangs Mother Purdy."

She moved pretty fast for an old broad, pulling a New Model .44 out of her boot and firing. Fargo feinted to the left and squeezed off two shots from his Colt, striking her in the left cheek and eye. She slid to the floor, shuddered twice, and mercifully died.

Fargo walked over to her and kicked her lifeless body off the stairs. Blood leaked from the holes in her head and puddled on the floor. He holstered his Colt and went downstairs into the cellar. Lila Mae lay dead on the dirt floor, two bullet holes in her heart.

Fargo sat down hard on a rickety old chair. He'd never felt so tired in all his born days. I'm gettin' too old for this shit, he said to himself.

12

By nightfall, the women had returned. The good folks of Flatwater set to the grim task of burying their dead and tending to the wounded. Jacob Belinsky had his hands full. He was assisted by Samuel Pruett Drinkwater, whose doctoring skills were surprisingly adept.

Mushy Callahan had taken a shot but it had passed harmlessly through his side. As he lay in a nice, comfortable hotel bed, he asked Fargo, "Did we get 'em all?"

"Yeah," Fargo said. "The Purdy gang won't be bothering people anytime soon."

"That's good," Mushy said. "I reckon I'm about to meet my Maker, ain't I?"

"I don't reckon you are," Fargo said with a smile. "Ol' Belinsky here fixed you up just right."

"Well it sure feels like I'm gonna die from all of this pain."

"It'll pass. Mushy—thanks for saving my life," Fargo said. "I'm obliged to you."

"Don't go thankin' me, Fargo. I didn't do it for you," Mushy said. "I did it for Flatwater. Town was good to me. I found a home here. Wanted to give something back, is all."

"You did that, and more," Fargo told him. "You want any whiskey?"

"That'd be nice," Mushy said.

Fargo asked Belinsky, "Is it all right?"

"It couldn't hurt much now," Belinsky said.

Fargo returned from the saloon with a bottle of the finest bourbon they had to offer. After Mushy took a healthy swig, Fargo grabbed the bottle and took a long pull. Belinsky had one, too. They watched Mushy die peacefully.

"Such a shame, all these good people dead," Belinsky said. "I don't know if this town will ever be the same."

"Time has a way of erasing lots of unpleasantness," Fargo said. "Flatwater will make it just fine."

Belinsky stuck out his hand and said, "If I don't see you again, Mr. Fargo, thank you for helping us with those terrible Purdy people."

Fargo took it. He said, "It was all in a day's work, Mr. Belinsky. Take care of yourself."

"You think I was planning not to?" he asked.

"I guess you'll be leaving now, won't you, Skye?" Sarah asked.

They were sitting on the church steps. It was almost midnight. The firefight with the Purdys suddenly seemed like a long time ago.

Fargo shrugged wearily and sipped some bourbon. Sarah sipped some, too. Fargo said, "Ain't decided where I'll go. Thought I might just stick around for a spell, at least until you find yourselves a new marshal."

"That's very thoughtful of you, Skye," Sarah said, a little dryly. She added, "All this killing . . . was it worth it? Just to save this shabby little town?"

"You may not see it this way for a spell, Sarah," Fargo said, "but yes, it was worth it. You may think this is just a two-bit town, filled with boring people, but those people had the courage to take a stand and fight. It's those type of folks that I like—and you should, too, Sarah."

They were silent for a few moments, then Sarah said, "You know what I'd like, Skye?"

"What's that?"

"I'd like you to take me home and make love to me," she said. "Nice, slow lovemaking, Skye Fargo style."

He stood and took her hand. She rose from the church steps, and together they walked back toward her house.

Nice, slow lovemaking, Fargo style. He thought, Why the hell not?

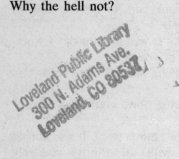

Utah Territory, 1858—
where greed is punished . . .
harshly.

"She's the purtiest thing you ever seen, Fargo. I do declare. I'd go so far as to swear it, but I don't cotton to such things. No, sir. But let me tell you, there's nuthin' I wouldn't do for her." Moroni Clawson hiked his feet up on a rock near the campfire, then leaned back to stare up into the clear, cold Wyoming night sky. The lanky man folded his hands behind his shaggy head and let out a gusty sigh. Skye Fargo waited for 'Rone to finish reminiscing about his fiancée back in Great Salt Lake City.

In a way, Fargo did not mind. If 'Rone kept talking, it saved Fargo from having to think up fancy new compliments telling how pleased he was that the army scout had finally found the woman of his dreams. Fargo preferred to stare at the same stars 'Rone looked up at, though he doubted he saw the same things. They had been on the scout for almost a month now. Captain Simpson at Camp Floyd had hired them to map out the trail already being called the Overland by many of the pilgrims flocking from back East and heading to Oregon. The army wanted the road both mapped and safe, to keep from spending all their time rescuing stranded greenhorns.

The land was beautiful, and that bothered Fargo. Not that it was the kind of land he appreciated most but that too many people moving through would ruin it. The night was serene. A lovesick wolf howled in the distance. Now and then the flutter of a bat sounded and its dark shape would block out some of the gorgeous smear of diamond-white stars arching across the inky sky. The spring weather was about perfect, a tad nippy but without a hint of storm in it. Just the way Fargo liked it.

And he was working to destroy it all by helping Simpson map the route to be taken by the sodbusters.

He heaved a deep sigh and closed his lake-blue eyes. Too many people spoiled everything. They dug up grassland meant for deer—and they shot so many of the grazing deer that the creatures vanished, either overhunted or having migrated to safer terrain.

"Been puttin' away everything the army's payin' me for my new wife," 'Rone rattled on.

"What are you going to do with twenty whole dollars?" Fargo asked. Simpson had not been able to pay much. Fargo and 'Rone had collected their full month's pay in advance since the captain wanted them out of camp. The rest of his soldiers had not been paid in over three months, although promise from the paymaster that scrip would be forthcoming always seemed to be for the following month.

"Twenty?" scoffed 'Rone. "Money like that's not enough for a fine woman like my Lydia. I got real money."

"Sure you do," Fargo said, smiling. He and 'Rone had partnered on and off for almost a year, and he had never seen the man with more than two nickels to rub together. True, 'Rone Clawson had vanished for a couple weeks before they met up again at Camp Floyd to take this mapping chore, but he had neither had the time to go far enough nor had he seemed any more prosperous after he got back. 'Rone refused to discuss what he had been doing, and Fargo suspected 'Rone might have another woman in the hills somewhere nearby. Maybe a Crow squaw he didn't want to talk about.

That might be why 'Rone spoke endlessly of his Lydia Pressman back in Great Salt Lake City.

'Rone pulled out his watch and held it up so he could see the firelight reflect off its battered gold case. For a moment, Fargo thought the man was going to open it to check the time. He had never figured out why 'Rone carried the watch or why he worried so much about what time it was in the middle of the night.

Excerpt from SALT LAKE SIREN

Fargo glanced at the stars and quickly estimated it was just past midnight. Although he could not figure out where so many of the constellations had gotten their names, and his imagination failed when it came to finding the outlines of strange animals and ancient people, Fargo knew the stars well. To the north around the two dippers ran the trail of stars he called the snake. Draco was its real name. And to the western horizon shone the smoky patch of stars called the Pleiades, near the bull constellation. The horns were easiest for Fargo to find.

But he didn't need a watch to know it was still a while until sunrise. Fargo saw 'Rone finger his watch, kiss it, and then tuck it back into his vest pocket.

"Got a picture of Lydia in the watch case?" Fargo asked.

'Rone jumped as if he had been stuck with a pin.

"No, nothin' like that," he said, sounding as guilty as a little boy with his hand stuck in the cookie jar. He put his bony hand over his watch pocket.

Fargo shrugged off the man's reaction. It didn't pay for partners to ask each other too many questions out on the trail. Besides, they were about done mapping the section of land Captain Simpson had wanted scouted, and it was time to move on. As much as Fargo liked 'Rone Clawson, it was time to head for the high country and enjoy all the joys summer brought. Alone. He wasn't up for the company of one man, let alone the hundreds to be found at either Great Salt Lake City or Camp Floyd.

"Fargo, I been meanin' to ask somethin' of you. A favor. You don't have to agree, 'less you want."

Fargo moved to the campfire and poured himself some of the boiled coffee. Whenever a man started out the way 'Rone just had, it meant trouble, and he needed fortifying from the strong brew. He took a sip, made a face, then nodded for 'Rone to continue.

'Rone dropped his feet from the rock and moved closer.

"You and me, Fargo, we hit it off good. Not just this scout but earlier, too. You're 'bout the best friend I got."

Fargo wondered if this was the right time to tell 'Rone he was parting company with him. He decided to wait a spell and see what the man was working himself up over.

"It's been good," Fargo said noncommittally.

'Rone sucked in a deep breath, then let it out in a rush, mingling it with his request.

"I want you to stand up with me when I marry Lydia. Fargo, I want you to be my best man."

"An honor," Fargo said, surprised. "Not one I thought you'd offer. You don't have anyone in Great Salt Lake City?"

"My brother Abraham died of cholera three years ago. John got lost. Reckon he's dead, somewhere up here in the mountains, since no one's seen hide nor hair of him in almost eight months. But that don't matter. I'm askin' you. What do you say, Fargo?"

"What can I say?" Fargo answered, knowing the anticipated solitude of the high mountains and camaraderie with wolves and coyotes would have to wait.

*   *   *

Astride his Ovaro, Skye Fargo felt as if he owned the world. From the way 'Rone looked around nervously, it was clear that the feeling was his alone.

"What's wrong?" Fargo asked. "You're jumpier than a long-tailed cat lying next to a rocking chair."

"Nuthin', it's nuthin'," 'Rone said. He glanced up into the hills above Camp Floyd and then forced his attention back to the broad dirt track leading to the army fort. Unlike others, Captain Simpson had not erected wood palisades around either his main building or the score of pitched tents. He relied on constant patrols to keep the Indians out and a knee-high fence to keep the chickens inside their compound.

A sentry waved to Fargo as he rode up.

"You finished lollygagging for a month and come back to lord it over us poor foot soldiers?" the sentry asked. The broad grin on his face showed he was glad to see Fargo and Clawson return. Anything that broke the monotony of pacing back and forth counted toward making this a good day. Or at least a better one.

"If you had any money, I'd swindle it away from you after a couple of hands of five card," 'Rone chimed in. "Bet you ain't been paid since we left."

"Good thing I'm not a bettin' man," the blue-clad private said, resting his musket on the ground and leaning on it. "I hope you got the trail mapped out real good so the paymaster can get a wagon in with all our money. They wait another month to pay us and we'll *own* the United States government, lock, stock and barrel."

Fargo had to laugh. Simpson may not have a good supply line, but he kept discipline and maintained a morale among his men that had to be the envy of any commander.

"We got the maps for the captain. Permission to ride on over and give them to him?"

The private snapped to attention and gave Fargo a mock salute.

"Anything that'll get us paid or laid, I'm for it!"

Fargo and Clawson rode in to the single wood cabin in the center of Camp Floyd and dismounted. Fargo stretched his tired muscles. They had ridden long and hard the past couple of days in order to get the maps to Simpson. 'Rone wanted to strike out for Great Salt Lake City right away to marry his sweetheart. Somehow, some of the man's enthusiasm had caught Fargo's imagination, and he no longer dreaded facing so many people in the city nestled beside the Great Salt Lake.

He might not have dreaded it, but he certainly wanted it over quick enough.

" 'Rone," he said as they went to the captain's door.

"What?"

"I don't have to dress up, do I? When I'm standing up with you?"

"Shucks, Fargo, those buckskins you're wearin' will be just fine. You might want to think on a bath, though. You're mighty rank after bein' on the trail so long, and I wouldn't want any of the other guests mistakin' you for a grizzly bear."

They laughed as they went into Captain Simpson's office. The young officer looked up, his eyes ringed with dark circles from the long hours. He was thinner than Fargo remembered, as if he had lost ten or fifteen pounds just from worry.

"Captain," Fargo greeted. "We got your maps done."

'Rone fished them out and laid them on the table. "You want to look 'em over? I think we done a good job. Leastwise, Fargo did. He drew 'em up real purty. I did all the dangerous scoutin'."

Clawson's joke fell on deaf ears. Simpson pushed himself back from the desk and rubbed his eyes, then turned his attention to the two men.

"Glad to see you're prompt," Simpson said. The sandy-haired officer unfolded the maps, then compared them with others done years earlier. For the next ten minutes, the three went over the places where the maps varied. The original ones had been drawn by John Frémont and lacked considerable detail. In places, Frémont had gotten the lay of the land flat-out wrong. This was the kind of information Simpson needed to shepherd the ever-increasing flood of wagon trains along the Overland Trail safely and successfully.

"That about does it, Captain," Fargo said when they had finished.

Simpson started to speak, then clamped his mouth shut. He sat down heavily and looked up at them. Fargo waited for the shoe to drop. The captain ought to be glad they had done their work and that he could send them on their way. Two fewer civilian scouts to pay had to help matters at a payroll-less Camp Floyd.

Fargo considered himself lucky Simpson had the money to pay them at all.

"What more you thinkin' on askin' of us, Captain?" asked 'Rone suspiciously. "Not more mappin'?"

"Not that. We're having problems with road agents. I can't find them in these mountains. Like smoke. They just drift every time a patrol gets close to them."

"What happened?"

"The best I can determine, a wagon was robbed about six weeks back. We just found the burned frame. Two men and a woman were killed. Shot."

"Could be Crow," ventured 'Rone.

"Not likely from the way the three were murdered. Indians would have taken what they needed and left without a trace. We found whiskey bottles and wasted ammunition scattered across the crime scene."

"You have other robberies?"

"A bad one earlier on. Lost a gold shipment, which is why I think they were road agents, stealing on their way through to other parts. My men have been watching the few bands of Crow hunters, and they've stayed well away from the trail and the settlers traveling through these parts."

"Then there's no problem," Fargo said pragmatically. "If the owlhoots have left the territory, they're out of your hair."

"I hate seeing unsolved cases. And I surely don't like the idea that I've exported problems I ought to have solved so that some other commander has to deal with them."

"If you don't mind my saying so, Captain, you worry too much," 'Rone started.

The young captain smiled crookedly. "You're not the first to make that observation. It galls me not to know what happened. I'd certainly appreciate it if you could track them down."

"A six-week-old trail?" 'Rone shook his head. "That's impossible, even for Fargo."

Fargo was not known as the Trailsman for nothing. He could follow a drop of rain through a raging storm. He could find spoor overlooked by the best Indian trackers. But this time he had to agree with Clawson.

"I'm good, Captain," Fargo said, "but I'm not that good. Nobody is. Be content these highwaymen are gone and let it lie."

For a moment, Simpson said nothing. Fargo read more to the story in the man's expression. The captain finally went on.

"I got two other bodies I can't explain. They were pretty well eaten by coyotes, so I can't tell how long they'd been dead. I'm thinking they might be linked to the others."

"Where did you find them?" 'Rone looked mighty apprehensive to Fargo, but Simpson didn't catch the anxious tone.

"Up in the hills above the camp. They could have been the road agents who killed the settlers. Maybe they're just another pair of names on a list of victims. And if they were the robbers, who killed them? Problem is, they look to have been dead for quite some time."

"Might be a band of outlaws had a falling out. Been known to happen," Fargo said, watching 'Rone more than the captain. 'Rone chewed at his lower lip and shifted his weight from foot to foot, as if he wanted to turn tail and run.

"Might be," Simpson said. "Not knowing is eating me up. I might still have an unknown number of road agents hiding in the hills."

"Let 'em show their faces, Captain," suggested 'Rone. "Don't go lookin' for trouble."

"I want to prevent it. That's my sworn duty."

"Well, Captain, as much as we'd like to help out by stayin' around, the truth is we can't. I've got a mighty important appointment to keep over in Great Salt Lake City."

"Oh?"

"He's getting married," Fargo said.

"To the purtiest girl this side of the Mississippi River. And maybe in all of the country," 'Rone said proudly. "Fargo's gonna be my best man."

Captain Simpson heaved a sigh, then rose and brusquely shook 'Rone's hand. "Congratulations. I wish you the best of luck. If you get tired of the big city, come on back. I'll always have a place for a good scout. That goes double for you, Fargo."

Skye Fargo shook the captain's hand knowing he wasn't likely to return. He was a good scout, but after he saw 'Rone Clawson married and settled down, there were other places to explore.

On his own.